"The way you loved your fiancée. It's beautiful. Inspirational," Adrienne said.

"I did what any man in love would do. When your heart is involved, you have no choice but to fight for your person, right to the end."

Your person. Adrienne wondered if she'd ever have someone she could really call her person.

She had trust issues now and walls up as high as the one they were sitting on.

"Don't you think it's strange how some people think loving someone is just a bonus in a relationship…in a marriage?" she said quietly, remembering her mother's letter.

"You're not being forced to marry anyone, are you? Someone you don't want to marry?"

"Of course not. There is no one."

She suddenly felt the fresh urge to tell Franco why there was no one, that she was destined only for another royal. She should help Franco on his way now, chase him away before her family did.

Maybe then he'd stop looking at her like…this.

But she liked it when he looked at her like this.

DIS

Dear Reader,

Here we are again at the start of another exotic adventure! This time, may I present a tour through Naples and beyond with our royal heroine, Princess Adrienne of Lisri.

Where is Lisri, you ask? Well, it's in my head, and it's a beautiful, wondrous place somewhere near Denmark, with mountains, fjords, pine-scented forests and a very strict, set-in-their-ways royal family who could do with shaking up a bit by the queen-to-be. Our heroine is determined to make that happen, whether she gets her man or not. (But let's hope she gets her man.)

I hope you're all enjoying a new season and new love stories, whether they're your own or in the pages of a good book. Now, off to Naples with you. Watch out for the scooters!

Becky x

A PRINCESS
IN NAPLES

—

BECKY WICKS

HARLEQUIN

MEDICAL
ROMANCE

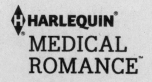

HARLEQUIN®
MEDICAL
ROMANCE™

Recycling programs
for this product may
not exist in your area.

ISBN-13: 978-1-335-40928-7

A Princess in Naples

Copyright © 2022 by Becky Wicks

Harlequin Enterprises ULC
22 Adelaide St. West, 41st Floor
Toronto, Ontario M5H 4E3, Canada
www.Harlequin.com

Printed in U.S.A.

Born in the UK, **Becky Wicks** has suffered interminable wanderlust from an early age. She's lived and worked all over the world, from London to Dubai, Sydney, Bali, New York City and Amsterdam. She's written for the likes of *GQ*, *Hello!*, *Fabulous* and *Time Out*, as well as a host of YA romance, plus three travel memoirs—*Burqalicious*, *Balilicious* and *Latinalicious* (HarperCollins Australia). Now she blends travel with romance for Harlequin and loves every minute! Tweet her @bex_wicks and subscribe at beckywicks.com.

Books by Becky Wicks

Harlequin Medical Romance

Tempted by Her Hot-Shot Doc
From Doctor to Daddy
Enticed by Her Island Billionaire
Falling Again for the Animal Whisperer
Fling with the Children's Heart Doctor
White Christmas with Her Millionaire Doc

Visit the Author Profile page
at Harlequin.com for more titles.

Dedicated to my travel partner in crime and fellow writer/sound therapist Farzana Ali. We may have the English Channel between us, but you're still one of my most royally excellent friends.

CHAPTER ONE

'*THE NAME NAPLES comes from the Greek Neapolis, meaning new city. Its close proximity to an abundance of interesting sites, such as Pompeii and the Bay of Naples, makes it a great base for exploring the area...*'

Adrienne Marx-Balthus zoned out of the audio guide in her ears. The woman in gold-rimmed sunglasses was still staring at her from the table by the window. Picking up her glass, Adrienne forced a smile in her direction. Of course she was going to be recognised here, too. Crown princesses like her didn't just leave their home country and turn invisible.

Still, this was rather awkward.

The woman pulled out a phone. Adrienne slid the earbuds from her ears as her heart started to pulse behind her blouse. It was one thing to be recognised, but to be photographed by a tourist on her first day as a junior resident doctor at the Cancro Istituto di Napoli wasn't ideal. Especially not when she'd already refused Papa's proposal of an official press photographer. Why would she want that? She'd come here to be...normal.

Signalling for the bill, she gathered her things.

Outside, the birds chirped in the trees and the buzz of the latte she'd picked up and brought with her propelled her through the streets of downtown Naples. Thankfully, the woman hadn't followed her. Running in high heels was not advised.

Papa's voice was in her head now, warning her that she'd be spotted in Naples, no matter what kind of white coat she was covered up in. Alexander Marx-Balthus, Prince Consort of Lisri, wasn't particularly thrilled about his only daughter—his wife's heir apparent—veering away from her monarchical duties for anything. Not even to pursue her career in medicine.

Adrienne sipped her latte on the move, taking in the piazza to her left, the way it smelled, the way the locals smiled. Everything was so vibrant here, colourful, promising. She wouldn't be dragged down by her own restless mind.

Her mother the Queen's quiet words in Papa's ear had allowed her to pursue this role and she would be grateful to her for ever. Her father would have much preferred her to engage in finding a suitable husband than follow a career, but that was not exactly at the top of her list of ambitions right now. At twenty-one, when she'd fallen in love with the dashing Prince Xavier of Molizio, she'd been too young to know better, and too blind to see through his cunning charade, as it had turned out.

Sometimes she still couldn't believe Papa

had encouraged her to go through with the engagement even after they'd all discovered what a lying, cheating… *No.* She frowned to herself. She would not dwell on that night at the Military Ball again; she'd done enough of that. But even after everything that had happened, and all the salacious rumours spread by the press over their sudden split, Papa had cited Xavier as an excellent match—in terms of his royal lineage, at least. He'd even told her that not everyone found love in a royal marriage, as though that was supposed to reassure her!

'I just won't have a royal marriage, then' had been her firm reply. 'I won't marry *anyone* unless it's for love.'

Papa only wanted the best for her, of course, she reminded herself…as long as 'the best' was someone with blue blood running through his veins, like Prince Xavier. Well, no chance of that here…

No chance of falling for anyone—not that I want to. It's going to be all about work, work, work.

At the other end of the piazza a line of scooters blocked the road, shoehorning into every inch of space around the cars. Gosh, it was hot here—hotter than at home in the summer, where Scandinavian breezes blew in over the mountains and cooled the rooms of the royal palace beautifully. But she pressed on.

If it were up to Papa she'd be letting her security guard, Ivan, take her straight to the hospital from her gated apartment, but she'd smiled and batted her eyelashes and convinced the man to let her walk this morning, saying she'd meet him there. It would be far nicer to walk and to get her bearings on day one, surely. Besides, her headscarf and giant sunglasses should hide her identity nicely.

Passing a dog straining on its lead to reach a fat pigeon, she let her thoughts run over her impending rotation again. She'd stood her ground at home, fought for the right to train as a doctor, and now she was finally away from Lisri and her royal engagements. At last some breathing space. There were no press photographers with her here, documenting her journey on yet another 'first day', which lifted her spirits again as the sea swept into view.

She must have walked uphill without realising. Inhaling the salty, damp air deep into her lungs, Adrienne flashed back to sailing trips on her yacht, *Amada*. One day, when she had some time to herself, which she knew would be rare, she'd take *Amada*, cast her sails again and conquer the sea herself. Ride the waves, the wild curves around the Amalfi Coast, out deep where the dolphins swam.

Dr Franco Perretta liked sailing too. She'd read it in one of his interviews in *Medical Heroes* magazine. For a second she thought of her new soon-to-be boss, sailing with her through caves, mooring at coves or in the shallows of secret bays. At thirty-one, she was still several years his junior—no thanks to spending time when she could have been focused on advancing her medical career attending silly social engagements instead, all while her family did their best to marry her off again.

It had only been a month or two after her relationship with Xavier had gone up in flames that her darling uncle Nicholas had received his terminal cancer diagnosis... But ultimately the tragedy had led her here, to this point. She hoped Franco Perretta would see and appreciate everything she'd had to overcome to get here, and not dwell too much on anything the press had written about her. They still loved to speculate endlessly about her and Xavier, and the fact that she'd been determinedly single since she'd broken up with him.

'Flowers, *signorina*?' someone called.

She bought the flowers. They'd look good in the hospital, all bright and cheery, signalling her new rotation and a new chapter in her life. As she walked, she felt a little nervous about meeting Franco Perretta in person for the first time. Had he heard about her reputation as Lisri's Ice Princess? Seen the stupid memes? Most people had. She was ashamed that such things had to follow her, but not ashamed of how she'd got the name in the first place. Of course she hadn't given any of those suitors a second more of her time than she'd been forced to give them by her family—they could all think what they liked about that. She'd got her studies back on track over the last five years, and her career came first now. With Dr Franco Perretta as her mentor she'd soon be in line for success on her own account—not because of her family name or their wealth or influence.

Would he be as charming as he'd sounded on the phone? Since first reading about him, and then talking to him about this position, she'd been putting a jigsaw puzzle together in her mind and filling in the pieces herself.

A thirty-six-year-old Florence native, Franco Perretta was undeniably the talk of the institute. And the country. And most of Europe. Franco had done more for cancer research and developing biotechnology in the last half-decade than anyone. Who else could she learn more from faster?

And Dr Franco Perretta wasn't just the cancer institute's senior consultant. He was a philanthropist. He'd joined the Cancro Istituto di Napoli after his fiancée had died. She'd battled a rare kind of cancer that had taken her life quite quickly. The exact type hadn't been mentioned in the interview she'd read, just the fact that no one had known enough about it at the time to tackle it easily. The interview had been more photographs than words, come to think of it, but it had sounded as if his tragic loss had been the foundation for a whole lot of gain.

Franco Perretta and the institute, co-founded by his father, the billionaire insurance tycoon Marco Perretta, were behind the research and development of almost every cancer-related drug the European Medicine Advisory Board had approved in Italy in recent years. As an aspiring oncologist herself, completing this rotation with Franco meant she'd be right on the front line of cutting-edge techniques, technologies and therapies. Thanks to all his connections, she'd also be involved in real humanitarian acts, and that was experience any medical leader should have behind her.

Even though all the females in her family had so far lived very long, healthy lives, Adrienne would have to take the crown in Lisri someday, and she wasn't going to waste any more time doing anything she wasn't passionate about. It might be decades before she stepped into the reigning role—her mother was only in her early fifties.

There was a screech. Adrienne stopped in her tracks. A scooter had collided with a car up ahead and she saw its rider, like a human-sized bullet, shooting from the bike to the ground.

She reached the scene to hear a flurry of Ital-

ian curse words and to see men with raised fists.
The guy from the scooter was staggering to his
feet, tugging at his helmet.

'Are you hurt?' She took his shoulders gently,
calmly. It was never good to raise your voice with
people in shock.

He blinked as if he didn't even see her. Then
a torrent of raging abuse flew from his mouth
directly at the driver in the car. Stunned, she
watched him limp purposefully towards his over-
turned moped, still yelling and gesticulating.

OK, so you're not that hurt.

'Princess? You're the Crown Princess, aren't
you? From Lisri?' The red-faced football-shirt-
wearing man in the car had stopped mouthing obscenities and was now striding towards her, one
huge step at a time. He'd left his car door wide
open, much to the annoyance of the other honk-
ing moped drivers. 'Your Highness, can I get a
photo? My wife is a huge fan.'

Oh, God, what now?

'Get on.'

The unmistakable voice came from behind her.

She spun around. There he was. Straddling the
seat of a matte green scooter—an MP3 Sport 500,
no less—was Franco Perretta. For a second she
just stood there, stunned. He was all man, wearing a fitted white shirt and an open leather jacket.
Taller than she'd thought, and utterly drop-dead
gorgeous.

'How did you…?'

'I was driving past. I saw the headscarf and I thought you might be trying to hide your identity.'

'Am I that obvious?'

'Get on,' he repeated.

She tugged the helmet he gave her over her head. The machine was more motorcycle than scooter, sleek and well-cared-for… Expensive. Her skirt was too long and close-fitting for her to ride a bike of any kind, but she didn't really have a choice. Squashing the bouquet of flowers under her arm, she yanked up her skirt and climbed onto the back behind him.

'Go!' she cried, pulling the tight fabric higher and hugging his hips with her thighs.

Mr Football Shirt was only a hand's grab away. 'Just one photo, Princess?'

Franco flipped the footrests. Her arms looped around his waist and she felt the flowers tickling her cheek between them. Only the helmet stopped her face landing smack against his broad, leather-shielded back as he put his foot down and sped from the scene.

A rush of heat and man and power and freedom flooded her senses as they left the crowd in the dust. In three seconds flat they were bumping across a cobbled footpath and skidding down a narrow alleyway.

CHAPTER TWO

'YOU'RE ABSOLUTELY RIGHT, Your Highness, there should be more of these in use around Europe.'

Franco had been listening to Irina, one of their palliative care nurses, agreeing with everything Adrienne was saying for the last ten minutes. It was almost as if she didn't want to risk any opinion of her own being something the Crown Princess might not agree with.

'If you need me for anything at all, Princess, inside working hours or out, I can give you my phone number...'

'You don't need to call me Princess, or Your Highness. No one does when I'm working. Thank you though, Irina—for everything.'

Adrienne was smiling kindly, but there was a definite weariness there. He could tell she was a little exhausted by Irina's attention, and trying not to show it. But Irina wasn't good at getting hints sometimes, and she'd been extremely excited about what she'd called 'the royal arrival' for weeks.

He listened as they spoke, pulling up the patient files he'd need for the rounds himself, trying not to let his eyes linger on Adrienne's profile.

A member of Lisri's royal family…here in his institute. She was joining his team for her next rotation and this was her first time living away from Lisri. He'd hired her because she seemed a good fit, and also, if he was honest with himself, because in between their phone interviews he'd been thinking almost non-stop about her voice— her Italian was tinged with a sweet, lilting Lisri accent and was sexy as hell.

It had crossed his mind that she might have chosen to live outside of Lisri as a means of escape. Drama seemed to follow her—at least as far as the media was concerned. But even if that was the case she was certainly proving keen about her rotation, and he admired a woman with an enterprising spirit.

Count Nicholas, her uncle on the Queen's side, had passed away from cancer of some kind. Franco assumed his death had propelled her studies up to this point, the same way it had compelled her country to donate generously to the Perretta Foundation on a regular basis.

She hadn't said so, but it was clear she was the driving force behind those 'Marx-Balthus' donations. The woman deserved her chance here. She'd worked damn hard. But all the staff knew that having a member of royalty on staff was not going to come without its challenges. People liked to talk about Adrienne. They called her the Ice

Princess of Lisri, he mused, still half listening to her conversation with Irina.

Allegedly, she'd given no man the time of day—not romantically, at least—since her break-up with Prince Xavier of Molizio a decade ago. Most people had assumed an engagement between them was on the cards, but it had never happened and the two had gone their separate ways. He hadn't paid much attention at the time, but he seemed to recall the press had written some pretty humiliating stuff about Adrienne that couldn't have been easy to deal with—especially at such a young age.

Irina was agreeing that Lisri was most beautiful in the spring, and that it had wonderful mountains for skiing, while Franco was appreciating the way the sun was falling like some sort of golden worship on the Princess's cheekbones. Before he'd met her in person that morning he'd assumed all those flawless photos of her had been airbrushed.

Ansell Ackerman would hit on her—probably before the week was out, he mused. The playboy surgeon wouldn't be able to resist. She was incredibly beautiful. She'd also just caught him looking at her, which made him square his shoulders. He'd hate for her to think he was yet another one of her adoring fans. He'd leave that to Ansell.

Giovanni the caretaker poked his head around the door and did a double-take when he saw her.

'Sorry, Princess…er… I left something in here. I will come back later.'

Adrienne fiddled with the sleeves of her lab coat for a moment, then crossed her arms and looked between Franco and Irina. 'You know, I don't expect any special treatment while I'm here,' she said with a slight frown, her head held regally high. 'I've had quite enough of that in Lisri. It's nice to be somewhere I can be normal for a change.'

'So we're just "normal" to you, are we?' he shot back as she rearranged a lily from the crumpled bouquet of flowers, now in a vase. They'd got pretty squashed on the way here, crushed between their bodies on the bike. 'You know, we usually try to be more along the lines of exceptional.'

'Which you are,' she said, narrowing her eyes in response, though he detected a hint of playfulness that stirred something at his core. 'Everyone knows that. Your reputation certainly precedes you.'

He sat on the corner of the desk. 'And it was your qualifications, Dr Balthus, and your passion that brought you here—not your family name.'

She looked surprised for a second, as if she really hadn't expected anything of the sort to come from his mouth. But he was damned if he'd allow her notoriety to preside over her work. The Lisri monarchy had ruled for a thousand years. It was amongst the oldest royal houses in the world. Her words and her presence could move mountains in any direction she chose, but right now she was here to work for him.

Why was he suddenly irritated?

Adrienne slid into a chair and her face was obscured for a second by the lilies. Maybe she'd anticipated how dull the residents' room would be. It was just an open-plan set-up, nothing special, several desks, a dull mud-coloured carpet that extended to the corridors outside. He'd wondered if she would want her own room, but her request was not to give her special treatment.

Not that it was stopping some people.

'It means a lot to me, being here with all of you,' she said now. 'This institute, this space. It's perfect—thank you. I can't tell you how nice it is for my first day here not to be filmed and documented for everyone to see.'

She sat back in the chair and closed her eyes, as if she was sitting on a throne for the first time…as was her destiny. Once her mother either stepped down or passed away she'd be right up there. Queen Adrienne. He couldn't look away from her serene face. She was going to be the most beautiful Queen there had ever been. Slim, but almost as tall as him, save an inch or so. Almond-shaped eyes the colour of a blue moon on the water, framed by pale expressive brows. Shapely, yoga-honed legs, soft as silk. He knew that; he'd felt them around his hips on the bike this morning, and he swore he could feel the imprint of them even now.

Irina had left.

'Should we go and do some rounds?' he suggested, suddenly feeling an urge to fix the lapels of his white coat. Then, 'I'll show you the assessment centre and the chemo suite—they're expecting us...'

Adrienne crossed her legs on the seat behind the desk and he caught the telltale red sole of a Louboutin and the flash of a milky pale calf.

There it was again...the stirring deep inside him, where nothing had moved for so long. Same as this morning, even before he'd had her wrapped around him on the bike. Instant attraction.

That's why you're so irritated. This is highly inconvenient. Why now? Why her?

'Dr Perretta, I really do have to thank you for this morning's rescue,' she said, swivelling the chair this way and that, slowly.

'It's Franco. And you're welcome.'

She stood up and crossed the room towards him, touched a hand lightly to his arm. The move made a swift knot in his stomach. 'I'm just Adrienne. And I really loved riding your bike this morning.'

He cleared his throat. 'You need a ride home?'

'No, I need you to help get me a bike of my own.'

He stood taller, thrown for a second.

'Or at least maybe you can recommend someone else who might help me get one?'

OK. This was interesting.

'I thought you didn't want any special treatment?'

'I haven't done anything that exciting in a while,' she said, dazzling him with a knockout smile.

For a second or two he swam in her oceanic eyes, waiting for his ability to form words to return.

He shouldn't be doing anything with this woman outside of work. His brother Benni would warn him about that. She was probably watched wherever she went, her every move scrutinised, which meant he would be watched too, by proxy. His worst nightmare. He'd always been an intensely private man. When he wanted attention for his work he knew how to get it, but his grief over losing Lucinda had only made it harder for people to get close to him, and he was fine with that.

There was something about Adrienne, though. He'd felt it during that very first phone call. Then her arrival had stirred him up for the first time in a long time…since losing Lucinda. And now that she was here, flashing that smile at him… Damn.

No, Franco, you will not be getting involved with her. Keep it professional… Keep your head on straight.

Somehow, though, for reasons he couldn't even comprehend, his mouth refused to co-operate with his brain. 'Let me see what I can do.'

CHAPTER THREE

IT HAD BEEN a long week for Adrienne. Her schedule at the cancer institute had been a whirl of patients and papers and research and administrative tasks.

Three mornings a week her day had begun with research working groups, rounds or academic conferences. On clinic days she'd typically seen her first patients at eight-thirty a.m., and she'd seen anywhere from ten to twenty patients a day.

And every time a door had opened and Franco had walked in she'd found herself holding her breath. Like now, as she waited for him in his office.

'*Buongiorno*, Dr Balthus. I mean Adrienne.'

He dropped a stack of files down on the desk in front of her and she wondered if he realised how gorgeous he actually looked with his touchable mass of midnight-black hair.

His broad shoulders looked like the perfect resting place for a weary head, and she'd noticed over the week that whenever he picked up a cup, or an instrument, or pointed, or gestured at a whiteboard or a screen, his muscles strained the sleeves of his white coat in the most delicious way.

'Our patient will be with us in a minute. I thought I should give you this first. Our next guy needs a smile.'

Franco produced a bright pink stethoscope from behind his back. He placed it before her as softly and proudly as he might the crown jewels, and she caught a golden glimmer in his green eyes as they trailed the length of her body, from her practical new shoes to her small stud earrings. He'd been sneaking glances all week and trying to be unobtrusive, but of course she'd noticed.

'It's pink for breast cancer awareness, but it also complements every white coat.'

'Wow. OK!' She looped the dazzling piece of equipment around her neck, still feeling his eyes on her.

'Looks good. As predicted,' he told her.

He had a way of saying a lot without saying much at all. While some people had been fawning all over her, acting as if she was some kind of celebrity they had to woo or impress, like that slick-haired sleazy surgeon Ansell Ackerman, Franco had remained casually on the sidelines, as though he was observing her from the outside.

He hadn't asked her one single personal question. Usually men couldn't wait to ask her about her life. She'd known she was beautiful since childhood.And in her late teens men would fall quiet when she entered a room, all eyes on her. They would talk at her too much, trying to catch her alone when they thought no one was looking.

Someone was always looking. Even here in Naples. Mirabel, the housekeeper, seemed to be permanently installed in her apartment, and Ivan was waiting outside the institute's gates right now, just in case she needed him. Luckily she'd grown quite adept at escaping such constraints over the years, much to her family's annoyance.

The sun was blazing through the window straight onto Franco's face now, spotlighting three faint freckles like a constellation on his left cheek. She wondered what his neatly clipped beard would feel like against her face. Soft and slightly scratchy, a tingle to the lips…?

The thrill of having her thighs around his hips on that bike had not yet worn off—she wanted more thrills like that. It was quite surprising, actually, the way he'd awoken something inside her that she hadn't even realised had been sleeping quietly. Usually the only men she met were those politely introduced to her by her family, who invariably turned her off before they even opened their mouths, but here was Franco, rendering her fascinated.

'I love it.' She smiled, only half talking about the stethoscope. 'People will certainly see me coming.'

Franco perched on the corner of the desk, the

way he did sometimes when he was reading patient files, and frowned at her. He looked like an ancient Roman statue in the sunlight. God, he was handsome. She'd promised herself not to think like this about any doctor, or indeed any man she couldn't possibly have, as what was the point in that? But all week, in every consultation, every talk, she'd been soaking up his words like a sponge and wondering if his heart was buried with his late fiancée.

'Are you having trouble out there?' he asked her now. 'Do people see you coming?'

'Of course. But at least I can run away faster now.' She gestured to her feet and the sensible trainers she was now wearing. Not her favourite style of footwear by far, but they were comfortable at least.

Franco laughed under his breath and drew a hand across his chin. 'That would be my worst nightmare…getting followed everywhere.'

'If I could keep things as private as you seem to, trust me, I would.'

She cursed herself under her breath. She'd pretty much just admitted she'd searched for him online and found nothing—which was the truth. Facts about Franco seemed to be as elusive as they came, but it only added to his appeal somehow.

'I liked the heels. Sorry it's taken me all week

to get back to you about the bike—things have been busy.'

Her heart bucked. 'Same here. It's no problem.'

Her eyes fell on the movement of his fingers under the fabric of his white coat. She pictured the two of them as they'd been on Monday morning, one hand on the brakes, the other firm hand righting her ankle when her foot had slipped from the pedal...

She knew he'd been busy, so she'd asked around about a bike herself. But she hadn't obtained one in the hope that he'd still offer his assistance.

'I've made an arrangement for you,' he said now. 'A bike I think you'll like. You can come and see it later if you're free after your shift.'

'That's...that's very kind of you. Thank you.'

Adrienne clutched the stethoscope between her hands as her heart thrummed. A bike arranged for her by Franco Perretta was exciting. But also risky for him, if he valued his privacy as much he seemed to. The paparazzi would have a field day, snapping her out on a bike with a handsome colleague. He must know that. He must be doing it to help her, because he probably suspected she was here to experience freedom as much as to learn from him and the team.

A gentleman. A gentleman with a heart and courage. How many girlfriends had he had since his fiancée, Lucinda, had died? She'd bet he could have any woman he chose—if he was even in the market for being with anyone. His mysteries intrigued her suddenly. She was envious too, she realised. What would it be like to successfully keep a secret once in a while?

'Where should I go if I make it out of here at a decent hour?' she asked.

Before he could reply, footsteps pattered down the corridor. Their next patient and a nurse. Franco moved from the desk at exactly the same time as she stepped towards them to go and greet them, and she almost bumped straight into him. She tried to move away quickly before embarrassment could flush her cheeks, but he caught her elbow and somehow her fingers rushed on impulse to his hair.

'You should watch your step,' he said lightly. She caught the gleam of desire and danger in his eyes right before he looked away, seemingly flustered. 'Even in trainers you're dangerous.'

Suddenly her heart was a crashing cymbal in her chest, but she swept back her blonde hair, rearranged her lapels, stood tall in his commanding shadow. She was here to work hard—not to get distracted.

But, seriously, why on earth did he have to be so damn attractive?

She stepped past him to the door. When she turned he was still looking at her like...*that*. She would tell him not to worry about the bike.

Maybe she shouldn't get involved with him at all outside work.

'I'll take you where we're going later,' he said before she could summon the words. 'Just give me an address and I'll pick you up.'

'I'll send it to you if you'll give me your number,' she dared, against her better judgement.

Damn it, I'm never usually like this with men. What is wrong with me?

He huffed a laugh that turned her heart into a circus. Then he took her phone and entered his private contact details. Had he planned for this to coincide with a Friday night? she wondered. Did he have any idea how she'd always had a thing for smart, altruistic types who gave nothing away about themselves when most men clamoured eagerly for her attention? The cool, calm, sexy, aloof ones were the only ones who had the power to hurt her, really.

Not that she was going to give him the chance to do that. This man was her boss and her mentor for a start. If her pride and professionalism were going to stay intact she was going to have to remind her libido that looking and not touching—not anything—was the best path to follow around Franco from now on.

Their patient was a forty-five-year-old male barrister, recently diagnosed with oropharyngeal cancer, whose name was Mr Geordano. She'd seen many patients like him already—wary, scared, sometimes in denial. She liked the way Franco was with them all: professional, kind, always letting them speak and shower him with questions before handing out calm, considered answers. No doctor knew the answer to every question, but he had answers up his sleeve for most things and she made an effort to remember all of them.

'This is an area of major research at the moment. There are several options available to you, Mr Geordano, and I'll let Dr Balthus walk you through her planned programme...'

Franco asked for her input a lot, she noticed, as if he was keeping her on her toes, and she was glad she'd paid full attention on the round earlier that week when the medical director of a centre for head and neck cancers had come to give a lecture. It mattered what Franco thought of her, even though she wished it didn't.

She was excited about tonight—to see him, to talk to him outside of work. To learn more about him...on a professional level, of course.

Maybe that would be enough.

Or maybe it would leave her wanting even more.

'What do you think, Pink Princess?'

Adrienne blinked. Their patient had addressed her directly, but both men were awaiting her opinion and she realised she'd zoned out momentarily.

Franco was shaking his head, and Mr Geordano's grey eyes said volumes even before he spoke. 'Here just for the publicity, are you? Did you run out of red ribbons to cut?' He turned to Franco. 'I thought you had real doctors working here...?'

Adrienne pursed her lips. She should have been prepared for this. The guy had walked in agitated and he had every right to feel anxious, but his fear was the kind that bubbled up and came to boiling point as an imperious rage. She'd seen it before.

'We call her Dr Balthus,' Franco said firmly. 'And I can assure you we only have the very best doctors on our team.'

'I'm still in training,' she explained to the surly patient, shooting Franco a glance that said *I can handle this.* 'And you're absolutely right, Mr Geordano. I am a princess. But it's a royal's duty to be perpetually in service, is it not? I'm here only to offer my knowledge and skill to you, believe me.'

She paused a second, then took a gamble.

'I lost an uncle to cancer, Mr Geordano. I have no problem admitting that his diagnosis changed my life. He's the reason I studied oncology, and the reason I'm here, trying to help as many people as possible to beat this disease.'

She cleared her throat, feeling Franco's laser gaze on her cheek. She'd mentioned her uncle only briefly before now, but his cancer diagnosis and consequent death had shaken her even harder than Xavier's philandering and the press's own interpretations of what had really happened between them. She wouldn't waste her life on worrying about the past when she could help better someone's future.

'Any royal obligations aside,' she continued, 'I consider it my mission on this earth to fight the fight for others who are enduring what he did—as a *real* doctor. Here or in Lisri. Anywhere the fight takes me.'

Franco's eyes were still on her. Had she said too much? She thought she caught a flicker of approval in his green gaze before he took over.

'I lost my fiancée to cancer seven years ago.'

Adrienne's heart jolted. His statement seemed to pulsate in the still air while their patient fell quiet.

'She's the reason *I'm* here.'

Franco's fingers intertwined—perhaps a sign that he was nervous, maybe not used to saying such things aloud.

'I started my oncology fellowship to understand more about what took her from me. Like Dr Balthus, I felt that was the only way I could get on with my life—to stay on this road, find better treatments, even cures. You see, you're surrounded by people who know the reality of what this journey is like, in and outside of this facility. Everyone here, the Crown Princess included, just wants to help you through it.'

Adrienne realised she'd been holding her breath. She blinked away a tear, which she knew Franco saw, and she didn't know where to look. She didn't quite know what to do with all this personal information, but their patient was now gripping his seat on the other side of the desk from them, looking between them.

'Thank you, Doctors, for your honesty,' he said, and Adrienne felt an immense rush of relief—right before the knots in her stomach rendered her breathless.

The way Franco was looking at his shoes told her he probably wished he hadn't said anything at all about Lucinda. It was quite clear he wasn't over her. Maybe he never would be.

Later in her apartment she looked less at the view of the glowing Mount Vesuvius, always on the verge of eruption, and more at her laptop, trying to find a photo. For some reason she wanted to see Lucinda. Franco was still grieving for her, even after all this time. Maybe he'd never got over losing her. When had he proposed to her? How long had they been together?

It had been her hope that seeing an image of Lucinda with Franco might help her to associate him with the source of his grief and his work here and cure her of this insane attraction she had before she saw him tonight. But she hadn't been able to find much at all. Franco was incredibly private, she reminded herself. Maybe he'd managed to delete any photos of them together, so they wouldn't mess with his broken heart even more.

She could relate to that, if that was the case. Even when she tried not to think about it she could still see him on the night of that hideous Military Ball, launching himself at the security team before they'd dragged him away.

Willing herself not to think about the past—not her own, at least—she went on with her search, knowing she should probably stop. This man was her boss, not some casual romantic interest, and definitely not someone to be sitting here wondering about.

But…

Did he miss Lucinda every day, or were some days better than others?

Experiencing pain like that had been bad enough over her uncle, she thought, feeling the little grey kitten who seemed to have adopted her on day one curl about her ankles. She'd named her Fiamma, the Italian word for flame, because of the little white patch of fur on her forehead that was shaped like a flame.

'But a partner, a *fiancée*…how would anyone ever get over losing that, Fiamma?'

Soon after, with the birds flocking to roost outside her windows, she pulled on jeans and a casual button-up shirt that she tucked in at the waist. Her heart pounded under her bra as she applied a deep maroon satiny lipstick, given to her by her cousin Emmaline, her uncle Nicholas's daughter.

'It puffs up your lips and turns you into a goddess,' she'd said.

Smacking her lips together, she wondered if she should be wearing it at all to go and meet her boss. Then she realised her jeans were perhaps a little too tight. In fact, her backside looked great in them.

Not good, Adrienne!

Maybe she should be wearing something less sexy—something that was more suitable for two colleagues meeting casually after work…

The doorbell rang.

Too late now, she thought, fixing a headscarf over her hair and sucking in a deep breath to calm her already frayed nerves.

CHAPTER FOUR

'It's a Vespa. Urban Club 125.' Franco patted the seat fondly, as he would a well-trained German Shepherd. To him a good bike was a man's best friend. 'About as safe and comfortable as you can get.'

'Not to mention stylish.'

Adrienne was obviously impressed. He watched her circle the bright red gleaming Vespa in the orange evening sunlight. Those tight blue jeans made her body impossible not to look at, but he'd have to try. He was her boss, her mentor. A fact he'd have to keep reminding himself of if they were to be spending time together.

He'd brought her to his sister Aimee's gated apartment and fetched the bike out of her garage, where she and Benni kept their collection. The Vomero neighbourhood was what you might call upscale, in a hilly part of Naples, with Vesuvius doing its thing in the background. His dad had a couple of apartments close by. His own penthouse was several streets away. It wasn't a surprise that Adrienne was staying in the exclusive neighbourhood too.

He'd heard her tell her security guard that she

didn't need him tonight, as she wouldn't be going far from home, and he wondered, as he recalled the frustration in the man's eyes, how often she managed to dodge her staff in order to have a little fun.

Not that this was a night of fun, he reminded himself. This was about getting Adrienne a bike.

But he'd been thinking about her a lot—especially after what she'd said in the last consultation. She'd spoken so openly about her uncle, and that had flipped some kind of switch in him. He'd talked about Lucinda too—not a lot, but more than he had in a while to anyone, let alone a patient and a colleague.

Even now he wasn't sure what had made him do it, or specifically what it was about Adrienne that had made him do it, but he'd told himself it wasn't an entirely bad thing that he'd let his defences down. He'd even felt a little lighter afterwards.

'Are you sure Aimee doesn't mind me using it?' she asked him now. She looked raring to go, straddling the seat in her designer trainers, her fingers working the clutch. She looked pretty fabulous on the bike, and he almost told her so, but didn't. What good would come from flirting with danger?

'Aimee's in Costa Rica till October at the earliest,' he explained. 'She's joined a conservation team somewhere in the rainforest, so she won't be needing it. If she comes back early she has more bikes to choose from.'

He crossed to the front of the bike, putting his hands over hers on the grips. He heard her breath hitch, saw her blue eyes searching his.

Damn, if she didn't rile up his manhood, looking at him like that…

He considered whether maybe he was a little starstruck around her. Anything was possible, he supposed, but whatever it was that had her constantly hovering in the corners of his mind whenever he wasn't with her would have to be stamped out. This was the future ruler of Lisri; there was no future for the two of them even if he *was* interested in a relationship.

Was she really such an Ice Princess, though? He thought about her warmth at work and couldn't help but wonder more and more about her past. She hadn't always been portrayed particularly kindly by the world's media.

'Brake. Clutch. Stop. Start. That's about all you need. And the lights are here.'

She flipped them on, dazzling him for a moment. He hopped sideways and she scrambled off the bike, flapping her hands around his face without touching him, as if she was more afraid of touching him than blinding him.

'Sorry! Franco…?'

'I'm fine,' he told her as her face came back into view. She was laughing now, just like he was.

Back on the bike, Adrienne rode a few more laps of the driveway, looking as if she'd never done anything as exciting in her life. What kind of life had she led before this? She'd mentioned a press team, who always followed her to official events, and he'd seen for himself the suffocatingly vigilant security guard who looked as if he'd follow her into a toilet stall if he saw fit.

He'd arrived at the idea, over the past week, from her few carefully considered words, that she'd been forced to delay her studies a lot, thanks to her royal engagements, which was why she was starting her last rotation at thirty-one. Also that it had taken her leaving Lisri to stop a persistent stream of titled courtiers from sticking their noses into every aspect of her life.

He knew practically nothing about her personal life in Lisri, and there was hardly anything online about her aside from a few mentions of her ex, Prince Xavier of Molizio, who'd recently had a third child with the woman he'd gone on to marry. It didn't seem as though she dated much. So, sure, he was curious about what had happened to put her off men back when she'd been barely in her twenties and he'd been in the thick of things with Luci.

But every time that curiosity got the better of him he reminded himself that he was dealing with the future Queen of Lisri, and it was probably not wise to ask personal questions. In fact, they could be followed and papped at any moment.

No, thanks. He'd had far too many people interfering in his life after Luci had died. They might have meant well—unlike the media most of the time—but it had made him tense, and even more angry. He still felt a chill remembering the reporter who'd shown up at his door one day, wanting intimate details of their relationship for an obituary. Benni had gone nuts. All Franco had wanted was peace and space to grieve.

If he was smart he wouldn't take Adrienne anywhere else... He'd just have her sign the insurance papers for the bike and take her straight back home. But then, she wouldn't have asked him so specifically about the bike if she didn't think he could show her where to ride it. And he was a gentleman after all.

She slowed the bike as she came towards him, stopping next to him. 'Where are we going now?' She revved the clutch with purpose and eyed him through the slit in her helmet.

He should say *nowhere*. He could already feel the sparks of something dangerous here—and what good would it do to blur the lines of professionalism with someone like her when it would only blow up in their faces? Losing Luci to cancer seven years ago, five long years after her diagnosis, had been pure hell, and Adrienne would be leaving eventually, too, going back to a royal life in Lisri that would never have anything to do with him. It would be just as final.

'Is there anywhere more exciting we can go?' she asked, still looking at him expectantly.

He pulled his helmet on, took his time with the strap, and zipped up his jacket, considering his options. If he took her home this early on a Friday night she'd know he was giving her special treatment. Making decisions for her, overprotecting her—wasn't that what people had done to her all her life?

And if he took her home he wouldn't know she'd be safe out on the bike—not really. Surely it was his duty to take her farther, to at least show her the roads.

What the hell?

'We should probably do a test run before it gets dark. I don't trust you with those lights in public yet,' he told her.

In Spaccanapoli the alleys were small. In the daytime they were crowded with shoppers, and stalls selling wares for tourists, and fruit-sellers and fishmongers. It was a little quieter now—the perfect training ground.

He told her she was a natural when they stopped at a red light, and when it turned green she sped ahead of him, grinning. She was deft and considerate, weaving through all the traffic they came across, so she'd probably be OK out

on the coastal roads…maybe after a few more
test runs. Those roads were as twisty as snakes
and the drops were steep. Maybe he should offer
to go with her…just the first time…just to keep
a friendly eye out.

'There's a route you can do through the Ar-
chaeological Park of Pompeii and the Vesuvius
National Park,' he told her when they stopped at
a water fountain modelled as a mermaid and took
off their helmets. 'It'll take you a whole day from
Naples on the bike, but it's the best way to see
everything you were talking about.'

He watched her mouth as she drank thirstily,
leaving no lipstick on the bottle. He liked the
shape of her mouth, the way it twitched when
she thought about saying something but kept it
inside instead.

'Unless you'd rather go by car…which might
be safer for you, I guess,' he added, reminding
himself not to look at her mouth, or even to think
about it.

'What do you mean? You just said I'm a natural!'

Adrienne turned her back towards a passer-
by who suddenly seemed to recognise her. Her
headscarf had slipped, and she hurried to pull it
back over her hair, resuming her disguise, such
as it was.

'I mean, you're *you*,' he said, moving impulsively to shield her, catching a nose full of her

enticing scent. It stuck in his throat, forming a new craving in the space of a heartbeat. 'It would take you a week if you stopped to talk to all your fans. We need you at the institute. Shouldn't you have security, anyway?'

She stepped away from his shielding as the passer-by hurried on, swigged from her bottle again, then wiped her lips with her hand. 'You heard me tell Ivan that you were my security to-night.'

He almost laughed. 'I'm not exactly used to watching out for paps, you know,' he pointed out.

He realised he should be irritated by her assumptions, but to his surprise he felt extra-protective as he saw her frowning eyes dart around, looking for protruding lenses. She was here under his guidance, so to speak. Of course he should look out for her—and not just at the institute.

'Not everyone's an adoring fan, you know,' she said a little wearily. 'And I don't deserve fans. I haven't done anything of merit yet. Not like you have.'

He dropped to the stone wall around the fountain, watched a pigeon peck the cobblestones by her feet. He wouldn't shower her with praise. Everyone else did that. No, he'd simply tell her the truth.

'I know you had something to do with your family's donations to the Perretta Institute after your uncle died,' he said.

She sat beside him, nodding, her eyes on the pigeon. He noticed a little engine oil on her expensive jeans, but she didn't seem to care. She'd been so enthralled with everything he'd shown her, all night.

'There are new drugs that went from phase two to phase three much faster because of your involvement…your interest behind the scenes. But you knew that, didn't you? You know you've done plenty of things with what you call "merit"—and not just because of some royal obligation. I saw how much this work means to you today…when you spoke about your uncle.'

He paused and watched her contemplate his words, still breathing in her perfume.

'There's a lot more I want to do,' she said after a moment. 'Thank you for your encouragement, though, Franco. It means a lot.'

'Do I sense that you feel there are some things you *can't* do because of your position?' He had to ask.

She pushed her honey hair from her face, tucking the loose strands back under her scarf. 'You mean apart from the fact that I'm followed everywhere and paraded around like some kind of poodle in a dog show whenever I touch ground in Lisri? If I hadn't fought for a real career before I take the crown I'd just be opening some hospital right now, instead of working in one.'

For just a second her eyes turned glossy and

hurt, and they pierced his heart before she looked away. Some protective urge made him want to pull her in and hold her close to his body, just like the thought of her plunging off a cliff on Aimee's Vespa had done earlier. She was so far out of his reach, though, he kept his arm where it was.

'I shouldn't complain about my birthright or the family traditions I'm expected to continue, even after what happened with Xav... I mean...' She sighed. 'It doesn't matter.'

He cocked an eyebrow at her, waiting. He could tell it did matter to her. A lot. She'd been about to mention Xavier, too. Her ex.

Franco frowned, wishing he wasn't itching to ask more. It didn't sit right with him that she felt inadequate in any way. Surely she could do a lot with the power she'd been given? She wasn't just a pretty face. She was clearly someone who made things happen. But what could he say? He barely knew her. She came from a whole other world, and however wealthy his own family was, she was way out of his league.

'You know what you *can* change, right now?' he said, getting to his feet as it started to rain.

'What's that?'

He pulled her up impulsively. She froze a second under his touch, and the wariness in her eyes made him drop her hands quickly. Too quickly, maybe.

'The fact that you've never had a *real* margherita pizza before—not till I've taken you to Riviola's,' he said, pulling on his helmet.

The whole ride to the restaurant he battled with his own brain. What was he doing? He knew he shouldn't extend their night, or even their conversation. Her security guy might have second thoughts about allowing her to run around without him and catch up with them at any second, meaning his own authority or motives might come into question. If her thin disguise escaped her again they might even be photographed together, which would not look professional at all.

But the distance behind her eyes just now had filled him with a crazy urge to break down her carefully constructed walls. One quick dinner. Then home, he promised himself.

CHAPTER FIVE

'IT WAS GOOD of you to explain your decision to work with us to Mr Geordano this morning,' Franco said, folding his tanned forearms on the table opposite her.

A waiter squeezed past behind him with three pizzas the size of steering wheels, but Franco didn't flinch. Thank goodness for the low lighting in Riviola's pizzeria. She hadn't much wanted to ride home in the rain by herself, so here she was, continuing the night in his company.

You could have handled the rain. You're just enjoying flirting with danger.

'There were so many other ways you could have coped with that situation. He was rude to you.'

'I'm used to it.' She shrugged, finding the salt shaker with her fingers, feeling his eyes hot on her. 'It wasn't about me anyway, Franco. You know that.'

'You're right,' he said, 'the man is angry at the world, and you were there to take the hit. You turned it around, though, and he left spouting praise about you. I've noticed that about you, Adrienne. You don't enjoy the attention, but you know how to use it to your advantage when it's necessary.'

She folded her arms to match his stance. 'I'm learning,' she replied, breathing in the fragrant basil and tomato air, trying not to let self-deprecation consume her. Her position didn't always give her an advantage.

'Well, from what I've seen at the institute, and on that bike, you're brave,' he said, and her heart contracted in a fluttery spasm.

Any compliment from this man seemed to lift her somehow, him being who and what he was: successful, admired, the sexiest doctor ever to straddle a Vespa. But all she could see now was the way he'd looked that morning, when he'd told them how Lucinda had been…maybe still was… the reason for his work. He was the bravest one of the two of them.

'I can't imagine what you must have gone through, losing your fiancée so young,' she heard herself say.

Franco tore his eyes away, and she cursed herself.

'I wasn't sure how to bring it up, or even if I should, but I'm so sorry for your loss. I could tell she's the reason for everything you do even before you mentioned her to Mr Geordano.' She put a hand lightly to his forearm and felt him tense. All muscle.

'She was only twenty-two and I was twenty-four when we got the diagnosis,' he said, looking at her hand as if it was a foreign object he didn't know what to do with. 'I used to wish it was me the cancer had got, not her. What did she ever do to deserve that suffering?'

'No one deserves it,' she replied softly.

'She was funny,' he continued. 'Right to the end. I mean, she had her dark days in the course of that last year, but mostly she was all light.'

'You were engaged? Why didn't you get married before she…?'

The question left her lips before she could recall it, but Franco sighed deeply and frowned.

'She was adamant that she didn't want to make me a widower. I'd only just proposed when we found out she was sick…and we weren't much more than kids ourselves, you know?'

He looked at her then, as if he was only just realising this fact.

'We were pretty young to get engaged, I suppose, but I was more impulsive then. She was smart. And brave. She accepted her fate maybe faster than I did.'

Adrienne sat back in her chair, listening intently as Franco went on to describe Lucinda in a way that caused the lump in her throat to disappear. Far from evoking more sadness, his stories about her made Adrienne laugh and shake her head, and try not to shed a tear, sometimes all at the same time. And the shape of his mouth in the candlelight made her long to taste his lips, as if she might absorb his passionate free spirit by osmosis.

She almost forgot where they were. He had a way of talking when he got going. His passion was enthralling and commanding. Fascinating.

Sexy as hell.

He wasn't only talking about Lucinda's illness either, as if he was determined not to let it define her. Instead he was sharing with her who she'd been before: a traveller, a fighter, an avid reader, a rememberer of everyone's birthday, an outspoken red wine drinker and a bad guitar player.

Hearing him talk just made Adrienne admire him more. Here was a man who was not afraid to love. He had more than enough to give. He *would* find love again. Because *he* was free to rain his passionate, all-consuming, unending love on whoever he wanted.

The rain was easing off on the windows outside, but somehow she could have sat there all night. Being normal. But just as she dared to think it she remembered she'd told Ivan that she wouldn't be going far and she'd been out for hours. He might be out looking for her even as they spoke.

'So, what about you and Prince Xavier?'

Franco's sudden question took her by surprise. 'What about us?' She sat up straighter, wondering what exactly he'd heard. The press had speculated to the point of insanity and published flat-out lies about why they'd broken up, but no one knew the truth about Xavier's affair.

Of course there had been rumours about him, too, but being powerful and male he'd come out of it in a far better light than he'd deserved. In fact, the press had glorified his next relationship, while she'd been left as the eternal Ice Princess for turning every other man down since. Infuriating.

Franco was looking at her somewhat sympathetically, which irked her. She didn't need his pity! She told herself to breathe it out, but thankfully their pizza arrived and threw a cheesy barrier between them.

He made a masterpiece of eating an entire slice without oozing one bit of sauce anywhere, and then he said, 'So, are you enjoying it here, far away from Lisri and whatever happened there to make them call you the Ice Princess?'

She swallowed. So he had heard, then. It was only to be expected, though. Was there anyone left on the planet who hadn't?

'Not that you seem particularly icy to me,' he continued, and she felt her shoulders square. His brow furrowed. 'I'm sorry you had to suffer whatever it was you went through, Adrienne. I don't expect you to talk about it, but like I said before, it's your work here we're interested in—not your royal name or your past.'

She lowered her slice of pizza to her plate, grateful for his words even if she did feel a slight twinge of regret that he was definitely only interested in her professionally. It was just as well, she reminded herself. She didn't need another man coming between her and her studies—let alone the one who was supposed to be mentoring her. But the way he was looking at her...

Why on earth was she halfway tempted to talk about Xavier with this man? Because he'd just talked about his Luci so openly?

That was different. Lucinda hadn't destroyed him willingly, or lied, or harboured secrets.

She must not be swayed back onto the subject of Xavier. Then she'd have to get into that night of their engagement announcement, at the Military Ball, when she'd gone for a breath of fresh air in the grounds beforehand, only to find him whispering with Contessa Estelle. She'd stood there in the shadows of the hedgerow, feeling cold to the bone at the words she was overhearing. It had become clear they were sleeping together on a regular basis.

She'd even heard Xavier admit to his lover that he had no plans to stop seeing her once he was married to Adrienne.

'We'll just be a hot secret, you and me. We'll go away together every other month, I promise you. Even if she finds out she'll never admit it. A scandal will tear the royal family apart.'

Estelle had challenged him, begged him not to announce the engagement, but Xavier had told her he was caught between a rock and a hard place. He'd wanted Estelle in his bed, but he'd also wanted the prestige of being married to the future Queen of Lisri.

Adrienne had never felt so used in her life. She'd confronted them both, of course, right there, and told him she was calling off the engagement herself.

She could still relive every horrific detail of what had ensued in the throne room, when he'd chased after her and in the face of her fury denied everything she'd told her parents.

'He knew I would never divorce him once I'd married him, Papa! He knew I wouldn't drag our family name through the dirt!'

Thank goodness her mother had taken her side in the matter and the engagement had never been announced. But even after Security had led Xavier away, still shouting obscenities at her... and even after one magazine had published the fact that Xavier had found her 'frigid and terrible' in bed, her father had had the audacity to suggest a reconciliation.

'Maybe you can work this out if you'd just agree to talk to him again. His family is a great match with ours, Adrienne. He knows what it's like to be royal.'

She realised she was biting the insides of her

cheeks again. And Franco was still watching her speculatively.

'I always had an interest in the biology of cancer, and I liked the way clinical oncology mixed pharmacology with the communication skills necessary to really connect with patients,' she said to fill the silence, picking at a fallen leaf of basil on her plate.

She sounded like a robot.

'I like to see how strong the patients are, Franco, how hard they fight and how their families come together when they're sick. You catch people in this time of distress and you can help to make them feel calm. You can make them feel cared for.'

'You're certainly good at doing that,' Franco said, but he was still looking at her as if he saw right through her, sea-green eyes penetrating every layer of her defences.

She shuffled in her seat, toyed with her napkin. She'd been babbling, avoiding getting back on topic, but he was astute…awake. Not easily fooled.

Franco served himself another slice of pizza and gestured for her to eat hers. He changed the subject adroitly, talking about his family instead. The Perrettas were an industrial, enigmatic bunch—from what she could garner from Franco, at least. They weren't aristocrats, but they were rich and well-regarded, successful, compassionate and driven. Franco's brother Benni ran Italy's second biggest automobile insurance company, and his eco-warrior sister Aimee was deeply into conservation efforts and community-strengthening initiatives. She was currently in the running for a position in Geneva as Environmental Affairs Officer with the UN.

Still, they weren't of aristocratic blood, she thought, picturing the stink it would cause in Lisri if she should start a relationship with Franco. She frowned fiercely. Why could she still not stop thinking about starting something with him?

Even as they made more small talk, about sailing, and Charles Dickens, the food in Sicily and the state of political affairs, their sexual chemistry sparked brighter than the candles between them.

'You're thinking. I can almost hear it', he said eventually, toying with a piece of garlic bread.

'I was just thinking about…the cat.'

'The cat?'

'Yes, Fiamma,' she lied, feeling guilty.

She just wasn't ready to admit how broken she'd been by Xavier's fetid, stinking lies, or how utterly embarrassed she still felt, knowing she'd been so infatuated with his handsome face and charming manner that she hadn't seen what was going on right under her nose.

It still stung that Xavier had only slept with her

to persuade her that he loved her. So maybe she'd been pushing people away ever since not just to defy her parents' wish for a royal wedding, but because she simply wouldn't survive if her heart had to go through something like that again.

'This little grey thing seems to have adopted me. I didn't think I'd be out this late. I should probably get home quite soon…make sure she's got some food,' she managed, fixing her headscarf again.

Suddenly paranoid, she hoped no one was taking any surreptitious photos that might somehow get back to her family. She imagined they didn't look much like colleagues right now.

'Someone else will feed her…don't worry. Everyone has about fifteen cats that they feed here. I'll get you home safe.'

She knew he would, too, but she was torn between the desire to be with him for as long as possible and the need to pull away, get back into her safe space and protect herself. She was starting to feel as if this was a date. At least that was what it might look like to outsiders. This was her fault. She'd done this, planned this, let the excitement of being with him override all common sense. Even when she'd sworn to complete her studies before even *thinking* about another man in a romantic light—especially one like Franco, who she couldn't even have.

Franco must have noticed her discomfort, because he raised his hand for the waiter. When he'd paid she felt that stirring take hold again—the fury over her Ice Princess reputation. He might not have thought it true before, but she was surely acting like one now.

Even so, Franco didn't need to know any details about Xavier, she decided. It wasn't as if anything was ever going to happen between them anyway. She wouldn't dare allow it.

By the time they pulled their bikes to a stop at her place, close to midnight, the tension between them was thicker than the jasmine-scented air.

'Thank your sister again for the bike, please. I'll be sure to take good care of it,' she said, squinting through the drizzle. 'I'm better with the lights now, see?' She flicked them on and off again, just to prove her point, and the soft huff of his laughter ruffled her nerve-endings. He seemed to linger a moment, immediately sparking all sorts of fantasies. If he kissed her...what would she do?

No. Don't even give him the chance. You would only regret it.

'Goodnight, Franco. Thank you for the pizza—it really was life-changing.'

Holding her head high, Adrienne steered the bike up the street towards her apartment and forced herself not to look back.

* * *

That night she slept fitfully. Her restless thoughts woke her up at four a.m., when she took a cup of coffee to the balcony and stared at Mount Vesuvius across the water.

Despite her disguise, she was still paranoid she might have been photographed on the bike or with Franco. She'd been reckless, putting him in a situation that might come back to bite both of them.

He didn't need to be dragged through the world's press because of her when he was simply a man going about his business—saving lives, for the most part. What kind of impact would the media's attention have on his considerable workload and the welfare of his patients? It would likely make him stressed and distracted. The man had something good going on and he'd worked damn hard to get it. And God knew he'd been through enough already...with his Lucinda.

Only Adrienne couldn't deny that she had badly wanted him to kiss her, to pull her in against his jacket, all leather and cologne and sexy Italian intensity...

No, she told herself again. She couldn't kiss her boss—no matter how tempting he was. It wasn't even worth contemplating.

His family didn't need her complicating things for them either. And there was Papa to consider too. He would cause a riot if he knew anyone had taken her out on a motorcycle—let alone some-one who was supposed to be a colleague and a peer. She'd come here to learn and to work, not to elicit another royal scandal. Her father still liked to think he could make his own rules for her, even now she was over thirty.

She suddenly realised she was simmering more than the volcano, just thinking about his auto-cratic decrees. It made her want to break every single one of the rules she'd agreed to live by. In that restaurant and out on that bike with Franco she'd felt that secret part of herself that had lain dormant for far too long getting restless again—like a lioness ready to pounce. And it had felt good…as if she was coming to life again.

It was not going to be easy, locking that part of herself away around Franco. But she had to. For both their sakes.

CHAPTER SIX

FRANCO WAS PLEASED to see that Adrienne was interested in the work being carried out in the chemotherapy day unit, and thankfully Irina had stopped being so starstruck. The team were now happily delegating duties and patient dismissals to her on a regular basis, and Adrienne handled them all with grace and gratitude. Everyone loved her.

Perhaps he'd been a little too quick to judge her before meeting her, assuming she was coming to Lisri for a new adventure away from home as much as for her work. She was early to every lecture, and he'd seen her hunched over a desk long after her shift ended on several occasions, working on treatment plans for patients. Her confidence and passion shone through every time she addressed him or the nurses, the surgeons, the radiologists and the oncology consultants. She was going all out to be of use and gain merit, and he was seriously impressed.

He realised he wanted to talk to her again— get to know the Adrienne who was still hiding beneath her professional white coat.

Ever since he'd taken her out to the restaurant

and lent her his sister's bike two weeks ago she'd been on his mind, slipping into his daydreams and his night ones too, if he was being honest. Maybe he shouldn't have opened up so much about Luci, but in a way he'd done it in the hope that she'd tell him something about herself in return. But she'd changed the subject—clammed up. He probably shouldn't have mentioned the 'Ice Princess' label they'd stuck on her. It was obvious there was more to the story of her and her ex than what had been reported, but it wasn't as if he could pretend he didn't know what people called her.

He made up his mind not to probe any more—he'd only be getting himself in too deep. Getting his heart involved was out of the question, especially under the circumstances, and he'd do well to remember that.

He found Adrienne in the residents' room fifteen minutes before her second consultation with thirty-seven-year-old data analyst Candice Trentino.

'So you're coming with me in case someone else calls me out for being a princess instead of a *real* doctor?' she teased as he approached her desk.

She was wearing her hair piled high in a bun today, and he thought again what a shame it was that she was forced to wear a headscarf whenever she went outside.

'Maybe,' he admitted. 'You already called me your security once.'

'Well, at least we weren't papped,'' she said before frowning. 'But just because you're paranoid, it doesn't mean nobody's following you. We should be more careful next...'

He bit his smile as she trailed off. So she'd been thinking about a next time too? He'd done his best not to imply there would be one. She was a closed book and the least available woman in Naples. He was here to assist her in becoming Lisri's best oncologist—that was all. Keeping her at arm's length was the only way forward... keeping her focused on her work, where her full attention belonged.

'I was impressed by this paper you wrote on the importance of evidence-based medicine in treatment decisions.' Adrienne tapped a printout on the desk as she swivelled fully in her seat to face him. 'Your passion shone through—which isn't usually the case in a medical or science-based paper. But then your passion seems to shine through most things, from what I've observed so far.'

'I'm surprised you've read that,' he said, pretending not to have noticed her compliment. 'I wrote that paper years ago.'

'I've read everything you've written,' she replied, as if he'd composed a book of award-winning poetry and not a collection of two-hundred-page documents full of charts and diagrams. 'Maybe I can pick your brain some more some time. I know you're busy, but I'd value your opinions, Franco. That twenty-four-year-old who came in this morning—Rosita Vettraino—the girl showing early signs of Ewing's sarcoma...' She paused delicately. 'I expected you to be present at the examination, but you weren't.'

'I know. I had to be somewhere else.'

He turned away from her as a rush of coldness ran through him like a wave. Even the mere mention of the rare cancer that had taken Lucinda from him could catch his heart off guard. He'd been bracing himself for this conversation.

'That's why I sent Dr Hernandez,' he said.

'He told me.'

He cleared his throat, turned towards the window. 'Did you get the MRI test results back yet?'

'Yes, and it's not looking good. Symptoms all checked out, so we've asked for a bone marrow biopsy. The family asked for you.'

Franco bowed his head at the palm fronds outside, as if sensing their judgement. He'd missed the appointment with Rosita that morning on purpose, accepting a last-minute emergency appointment in the radiation room instead. He wasn't proud of himself.

When it came to Ewing's, he was more than on

top of current research and treatments, but meeting any woman who was even so much as *suspected* of suffering the rare form of cancer always felt a little too close to home. He'd seen Rosita's file. He would meet the young woman soon. But he was stalling and he knew it.

His researchers had successfully reduced tumour growth in young patients just like her with a new biotech drug, but the trial was still stuck in phase two, bound up in legal procedures. They needed phase three status so they could take on more patients—so they could start offering more hope to people like Rosita and her family. His lawyers kept saying it was only a matter of weeks until phase three was approved, and he wanted—needed—to deliver better news than he currently had.

Adrienne was looking at him curiously. He knew he hadn't mentioned to her the kind of cancer that had taken Luci when he'd talked about it before.

Ewing's sarcoma was a very rare type of tumour that grew in the bones—or, in Luci's case, the cartilage and nerves around the bones. He'd watched it snatch her away, all of her—her energy, her tireless drive… And the beautiful body he'd worshipped for several years of his young adult life had been reduced to a brittle shell. He'd watched her crumble on the inside too—watched the sparks fade from her eyes and listened to her crying late into the night towards the end. Not out of fear of dying, but out of sadness at leaving *him* behind. They'd only released her from the hospital in Rome so she could come home to die...

'In the case of Lucinda it spread to the lungs before it was even diagnosed,' he murmured, lost in thought.

Adrienne's neat eyebrows shot up. 'Lucinda had Ewing's? Franco, I didn't mean... You don't have to...'

'As you know, it usually affects people between the ages of ten and twenty. Luci was a rare case, contracting it in her early twenties like Rosita.' He paused to meet her eyes finally. He saw sympathy pulse in her pupils, but he didn't want it. 'There are new forms of treatment, Adrienne— more since I wrote the paper you read. The drugs currently in trial are the ones we need.'

'What trial?'

He paced the room, still lost in thought. 'One patient out of two hundred had an adverse reaction to the drug and the whole damn thing got put on hold. I offered to give them whatever they needed to launch phase three through the Perretta Institute, but it's not about the money—it's more bureaucratic red tape holding things up as usual, while people suffer.'

He paused.

'My first thought when I heard about Rosita was that we have to get the trial moving again.

Just one cycle of this drug could reduce the cancer's spread to other parts of her body in weeks. This is a revolutionary advancement, Adrienne, and it will make a difference to so many others too. The authorities know it's big—that's why they're being extra-vigilant about it—but we're running out of time to help Rosita...'

'What do we have to do?'

He frowned. It wasn't easy to expedite things like this. 'I don't know,' he admitted. 'But I can't stand watching people suffer when they might not have to. I've already been on the phone personally to everyone I can think of—several times.'

He busied his fingers with the patient file on his clipboard, aware of the way she was still studying him thoughtfully. Shame rippled through him at the memory of avoiding the consultation that morning even now, as he talked about the promising drug, the kids and adults it had already helped, and what it could do in the future. He knew he was the most knowledgeable medic on Ewing's in the entire institute.

But this wasn't all about waiting for the trial. He couldn't talk about this specific rare cancer without bringing Luci up—and remembering everything they'd gone through in their battle to fight that soul-sucking disease. The work he'd launched himself into because of Luci kept him going, and kept others going too, even when he rarely spoke about her. But Adrienne hadn't even

mentioned her before he'd cut in at Mr Geordano's consultation. What had he been thinking,
making this all about himself and Luci when it
wasn't about them at all? He was here to do a job.
That had burned in his mind all day as he went
about his duties.

He had no intention of letting his attraction to
Adrienne affect his work in any way, but already
he was finding it hard to concentrate on what
he should be doing—and he'd spoken too much
about Luci in front of Adrienne.

He hadn't looked at his photo album in weeks,
either. Those memories of him and Luci were
in a box under his bed and he hadn't pulled it
out, trying to wish her back to life, since Adrienne had started working here. Unlike what he
had done after several disappointing dates with
other women.

He hadn't exactly been a paragon of virtue
since Luci had died. She'd made him promise
he wouldn't become a monk, and there had been
a few women at first… OK, maybe more than a
few women, when he'd needed to bury his grief
and loneliness for even a handful of minutes. The
brief relationships he'd managed after that had
been little better. He'd felt numb, and he knew
he'd given women the impression that he was
aloof and emotionally unavailable. He hadn't
cared if they stayed with him or not.

So why was his heart refocusing now—slowly,

like a squeaky old camera lens—on the one woman he couldn't ever have? The Crown Princess of Lisri. What kind of card was the universe dealing him now?

His insides gnawed at each other like starving animals as they walked in silence to the chemo lab, and before his thoughts could spiral any further their patient arrived, dressed all in black, just like her mother. As they ran through copies of Candice Trentino's scans, X-rays, CT scans and pathology slides in the lab's all-white consultation room Franco tried to keep his eyes from Adrienne's as Candice's mother began to weep.

'It's a frightening situation when you're waiting for results like you have been,' Adrienne empathised.

He watched her pour a glass of water for both women. The white-painted room was made less stark by the platitudes printed and framed on the walls, but he knew nobody could focus on anything for long in this room. In this situation. Most people left loathing it—at least the first few times.

'We've examined the cells and tissues from your liquid biopsy earlier this week, and it seems that what we're dealing with is a pre-cancerous condition of the larynx,' Adrienne explained gently.

'You mean I might get throat cancer?' Candice

croaked, squeezing her mother's hand. 'I don't even smoke!'

'But you do drink too much—I've always said that,' her mother cut in. 'That can't be good for her, can it, Doctors?'

'You try working where I work!' Candice exclaimed, pulling her hand back.

For a second she put her head between her knees, but it was her mother who started gasping for breath. Candice reached for her hand again, gripping it tight like a steel vice.

Franco caught Adrienne's glance. Patients sometimes acted stronger than their family members at first, but he knew discussing a new diagnosis could affect people differently.

Bad news was unstoppable—like a rampant bull you wanted to run from but couldn't. It pinned you down, then stamped on you over and over again whenever you tried to get up. Luci had been shell-shocked at the time, almost deaf to her diagnosis. Later, in a heap on the bathroom floor of a hotel in Rome, the full extent of it had struck her. Her sobs had racked the entire corridor, and someone had even knocked on their door to check no one had died.

'Not yet!' Luci had replied.

Typical Luci. He'd tried so hard to be the strength she needed, but he'd never felt as strong as he'd looked.

He scanned the slides, wishing he could shake

off his earlier conversation with Adrienne about Rosita and Ewing's sarcoma. It was his job to be everyone's strength now, and Adrienne must think him completely unprofessional for sending another doctor to that consultation earlier.

Adrienne was still talking. 'There are plenty of treatment options these days, of course, which we'll run through with you if you feel up to it…'

Candice was shaking her head. 'I can't do chemo,' she said adamantly. 'I can't lose my hair.'

'You might not have to.'

'I don't want to take any drugs.'

'It might not come to that either, Candice,' Franco said gently. 'There's now immunotherapy treatment, which we call biologic therapy,' he explained. 'The treatment uses your own immune system, your body's natural defences, to fight the tumour…'

They had both women listening attentively for the duration of the appointment. But the second they were alone Franco pulled Adrienne aside before she could leave. He knew his mind would keep spinning over their new Ewing's sarcoma patient unless he talked it over with Adrienne first.

'I need to talk to you tonight, if you're free,' he told her.

CHAPTER SEVEN

THERE WAS A letter waiting for her on the door-mat. After showering the day off her, she opened it out on the balcony, feeling her heart pound in anticipation as she slid a nail under the scarlet wax crest. Her mother the Queen still insisted on sealing all her letters with it.

> *My darling,*
> *I hope this finds you somewhere peace-ful. I've been thinking of you fondly over the past few weeks...the royal palace feels empty with you gone.*
> *I trust you are taking some time for your-self and enjoying the sights of Naples—it was always a secret dream of mine to travel for an extended period outside of Lisri.*
> *I know I don't tell you this often enough but I'm proud of you...*

Adrienne was startled as a silky swish of warmth curled around her ankles. She lifted Fiamma onto her lap and shook off her shoes, then read the last sentence again, picturing her moth-er's wise eyes and soft, kind face.

A pang of guilt struck her from nowhere. She herself was living a dream that her mother, Lisri's own Queen, had been forced to abandon when she'd married Papa when she was twenty-one.

Not that they hadn't been in love. Her parents had been smitten the moment they'd set eyes on each other, so the marriage arrangement had been welcome when it came some six months later. Even so, Adrienne was coming to learn with age that her mother harboured certain regrets about marrying so young and having to assume the crown without having done anything for herself first.

I've been inspired by your adventures, Adrienne, so I've been in the kitchen again. Chef Maxy was very surprised when I offered to help her bake—it's been so many years, you know. But it's something I dared to dream I might have done for a living, had I not been so fortunate as to be born a future monarch, and we made the most wonderful cake together. In fact I might even make another one when you come home for the polo match.

I also write to tell you, Adrienne, that Baron Vittorio La Rosa of Laughterhaven South will be in Naples next month, to visit the Military Academy. I happened to men-

tion you were there and that you might be interested in showing him the sights of the city.

I wouldn't suggest this if he wasn't a handsome single man, my darling. I'm sure I don't need to mention that we'd be thrilled to unite the La Rosa and Marx-Balthus families...

There she goes again. Adrienne slapped the letter to the table and pressed her nose to Fiamma's fuzzy head to calm herself. Just as the Queen was confessing how she might actually find her daughter's ambition an inspiration, there she went, attempting to matchmake in the hopes that Adrienne might fall in love on the spot and drop everything to return to Lisri, get married and start making babies.

As if.

But, then again, if I could feel anything like I felt when I first saw Franco for someone who wouldn't cause the kingdom to collapse, maybe I wouldn't be entirely opposed to getting married soon...

Her phone pulled her out of her dream.

Franco was here.

She'd told Security to give her a missed call when he was downstairs, signing in.

Even knowing he was in the building sent her temperature rising.

The purring grey cat sprang from her lap onto the marble tiles as Adrienne hurried for her bag.

Smoothing down her dress, she made for the elevator.

He had asked if she would meet him tonight but hadn't said why, or where they were going. Every attempt made by her head to say no had been pummelled into submission by her heart.

Franco's eyes trailed her up and down, burning like coals from Vesuvius, as she climbed off her bike and unfastened her helmet, shaking her hair free before tying on a headscarf.

Again, she felt empowered by his appraising glances but wished she didn't still feel as if she was walking a dangerous line towards some un-mitigated disaster. Her wild heart kept bashing her ribs in a way it had never seemed to do for any of her parents' set-ups, and it would probably never beat the same way for the Baron her mother had promised she'd spend some time with.

Her mother's letter had really got under her skin, but she had to forget it and try to enjoy to-night. It wasn't as if this was a date anyway—just as the last time they'd gone out together hadn't been a date.

Or *was* this a date?

'This place is stunning,' she enthused, taking in the view.

He'd brought her to Castel dell'Ovo, the old-est castle in Naples, rising like a sandy fortress on a peninsula called Megaride. The waves were crashing in the distance and a sea breeze softened the heat. Every boat on the ocean ahead of them created a riot of colour, like the flowers around them on the hillside.

Franco extended a hand to lead her down a stony staircase. 'Welcome to the first inhabited centre of ancient Neapolis,' he said.

His shirtsleeves were snug around his biceps, and he wore navy-blue board shorts that came to just below his knees. He had really strong legs—from hiking, she'd heard him say once. She'd bet he'd like the scenery in Lisri, as her island nation, off the Danish coast, was at its best in summer, and the hikes out into the mountains and fjords were breathtaking.

Franco was smiling as she reached the bottom step. For a moment she was so entranced by the sight of him against the rolling ocean waves, and daydreaming of him hiking with her in Lisri, that she almost forgot to appreciate what he was actually showing her.

A three-hundred-and-sixty-degree panorama of the sunset across the gulf smiled before her, with the city sparkling in golden light.

'It's beautiful,' she breathed, just as her eyes landed on his. The deep green hue reminded her of home, of all the colours of new things born in the spring.

'It certainly is.'

He almost sighed, and he was still looking at

her. Persistent butterflies assaulted her stomach as she became aware that he was looking at her long, slim legs in the short light blue sundress she wore. She'd opted to wear it so she could easily ride the bike…but she couldn't deny how it thrilled her to see him looking at her and clearly liking what he saw.

He led her along the seafront in front of the castle and set his backpack down on the sweeping stone wall. There were a couple of people lingering up ahead, pointing cameras at the views, but thankfully no one close enough to recognise who she was.

'Just us,' he said, as if reading her mind, and she sat beside him on the wall, daring to push back her headscarf a little and swinging her legs towards the sea about ten feet below. 'Well, just us and your security.'

Franco nodded towards where Ivan had positioned himself in the shade, several feet away, fanning his face with a pamphlet. Too far away to hear their conversation, thankfully.

'Ignore him,' she said.

Summer air blew warm about her cheeks, playing with her hair, blowing strands against his shoulder, which he may or may not have noticed. She wanted to feel 'normal' again, but she was starting to realise that maybe she'd never feel normal around this man.

He poured them each a glass of something

sweet and cold, and told her a legend about a siren who'd landed here and given a name to the ancient city, the first settlement of the Greeks.

Franco was different from the Italian men in Naples, she thought. In her opinion guys from Florence were far more attractive, and he was the cream of the crop—the foam in the cappuccino. Exactly her type, she realised.

Funny… She'd never even thought she *had* a type till now.

It was clear he worked out from his impressive muscular physique. Not like most of the men who peacocked around her normally, who thought their money and their status could buy them every woman's desire and wouldn't know a barbell if it hit them on the head.

He could kiss her now, she realised. She'd be powerless to resist. She stifled a giggle. She really should start reading more than romance novels and medical journals, she decided.

Then he spoke.

'I have to tell you something.'

His eyes on the sea made her stomach lurch.

'That appointment today…the girl with Ewing's sarcoma…'

She nodded. Of course he would bring that up. 'I'm so sorry I mentioned you not being there,' she said. 'I didn't know it was Lucinda's diagnosis…'

'How could you have known?' He cut short her

profuse apology with a wave of his hand. 'I didn't attend it on purpose, Adrienne, and not just because I'm waiting for the trial. It was selfish of me not to go. I know I painted a happy picture of her before, because that's the Luci I like to remember, but that doesn't mean I enjoy talking about what happened to her in front of everyone. However, I'd like you to understand.'

He met her eyes, and she knew he meant he wasn't comfortable talking about it with *her*.

'I do understand,' she said, even as her heart's own beat skipped away from her.

His knuckles turned white as he gripped the wall between them. 'Ewing's sarcoma…the type of cancer she had…it's so rare. The fevers and the pain in her bones were unbearable…' He trailed off a second, and she saw his Adam's apple quiver in his throat—just before she noticed Ivan, motioning for her to put her headscarf back on properly.

'There was only one treatment protocol for first-time patients when she got sick,' Franco went on. 'And because it's most commonly found in adolescence, and mostly considered a paediatric cancer, she was treated at a children's hospital in Rome. We spent *months* there—and I hate Rome. The food there is all tourist food…it was better in the hospital—which was the only good thing about it.'

Adrienne followed his gaze out to sea, wishing

she knew what to say. This was an unprovoked outpouring she hadn't expected. It made her want to loop a comforting hand around his, but she busied her fingers with her headscarf.

To her surprise, once she'd finished, Franco took her hand. He gripped it like a vice, almost as though he were absorbing some kind of strength from her, and then he relaxed his hand in hers. It felt natural to touch him, she observed, looking at her slender fingers entwined with his. It also made her heart pound harder...

'Unfortunately, the type of chemo they used for Ewing's at the time meant Luci had to be an inpatient for longer than usual. She had an infusion every two to three weeks. Sometimes she was in there up to six days at a time. She wasn't too enthusiastic about being treated alongside children, as you can imagine. But the care she received and the atmosphere on the ward was better there than anywhere here. Not that it did much good in the end.'

'I can't imagine what you must have gone through,' Adrienne managed.

Then Franco told her all about the treatments they'd tried, and the researchers he'd gone to meet—even the week they'd spent in the Amazon, drinking a potent tribal brew called *ayahuasca*, just in case they could coax the demon out with magic. He'd done everything in his power to try and save his true love, and he hadn't given up or fled in the face of adversity. He really was the very best kind of man. The kind you could fall for hard and for ever, she thought to herself.

'The way you loved her… It's beautiful. Inspirational,' she said aloud.

He shrugged and dropped her fingers, turning his face to the sky. 'Not really. I just did what any man in love would do. When your heart is involved you have no choice but to fight for your person—right to the end.'

Your person. Adrienne repeated it to herself, wondering if she'd ever have someone she could call her person. She had trust issues now—and walls as high as the one they were sitting on.

She watched a seagull swoop for a fishing boat. 'Don't you think it's strange how some people think loving someone is just a bonus in a relationship…in a marriage?' she said quietly, remembering her mother's letter.

'What are you talking about?'

She closed her eyes, embarrassed. 'I don't know…'

Franco frowned at her. 'You're not being forced to marry someone, are you? Someone you don't want to marry?'

'Of course not. There's no one.'

Franco tossed a pebble over the edge and they watched it drop into the water.

'But my family *has* been quite adept at making

strategic marriage connections over the years,' she continued thoughtfully. 'Maybe that's why I'm such a disappointment to everyone.'

She bit her lip, knowing she had a habit of revealing too much when she was nervous. But she suddenly felt a fresh urge to tell him *why* there was no one, to tell him that she was destined only for an aristocrat, even if her helpless heart should start yearning for someone else entirely. She should help Franco, she thought. Chase him away before her family did. Maybe then he'd stop looking at her like...*this*.

But she liked it when he looked at her like this.

'I won't claim to have any idea of what your life must be like in Lisri, but I *do* know that you're in my country now,' he said, nudging her gently as the breeze toyed with his hair, making her want to touch it. 'You're in my castle now—and in *my* castle you can never be a disappointment.'

She leaned into his shoulder, stealing a lungful of his scent.

'I'm sorry if I spoke too much about Luci,' he said. 'I just wanted to get everything out there, you know, in case any questions about her or her treatment come up with Rosita's family. A lot of people don't know me, or why I do the work I do. But some do...'

'I'm honoured to be one of those people,' she replied truthfully. 'For what it's worth, I know

Ewing's sarcoma patients are rare. You're probably never going to be ready to see its impact on anyone else. But you will still be the best person in that room. People need a heart like yours, Franco. As well as your experience. And I'm here now. And I'm going to help you get that trial to phase three so Rosita can have the help she needs.'

An idea was forming in her head already... It would potentially ruffle some feathers in Lisri, but she was determined.

'We'll find a way to get it approved.'

Her breath caught as he brought her hand to his lips, letting them linger against the back of her fingers for a moment. The ground could have opened up and she wouldn't have noticed. She knew Italians kissed people's hands and cheeks all the time, but this gentle touch felt entirely different. He could kiss her lips right now... Was he thinking about it, just as she was?

'Has no one else proposed to you since Prince Xavier?' he asked her quietly, his green eyes slanted.

The question made jelly of her whole body. She shook her head, feeling her steady composure evaporating on the spot.

'I'm the Ice Princess, remember?' she told him, and she watched him visibly withdraw. She could have kicked herself. She'd completely ruined the moment.

* * *

Back at the end of her driveway later, Franco didn't get off his bike and he left the engine running even as her apartment keys burned in her pocket once again. Ivan pulled up on his bike just after them, and thankfully disappeared into the building.

'Thanks for letting me explain myself tonight,' Franco said, scanning her eyes through the gap in his helmet.

'I told you, it's OK.'

Her mind was a hurricane. He hadn't kissed her when he could have done. He'd asked her again if there was anyone, then left her hanging—as if waiting for her to elaborate, or kiss him first. Of course she hadn't. She'd let the moment linger and pass them both by, until he'd quietly suggested they ride home. Then again, knowing Ivan was several feet away, watching them, would have killed the moment even if she hadn't done it first.

'You're a good listener.'

'Well, you're even better at talking, so I guess we're a good match.'

She berated herself even as he muttered a laugh. *Why did you say that?*

Her brain was on overload. The night air felt thick with anticipation. Maybe he was waiting for her to make a move, she thought. She was royalty, after all, and he was nothing but respectful.

Rattled, she stalled her bike's engine by mistake. And in the end he took the pressure off in the simplest way.

'*Buona notte*, Adrienne.'

She watched him peel away into the night and felt as if something had ended before it had even started.

All night the fire in her veins burned hotter, as if she could feel the curse of her own royal blood working its evil magic.

He probably sensed she'd only bring trouble to his door, and he was right. She didn't give her past away easily, and neither did she put her emotions on display, where they could be scrutinised and judged. Franco, in spite of being a very private man, was trying to invite her in, gradually sharing parts of himself, while she kept shutting him out. Maybe *that* was why he wouldn't kiss her.

It didn't matter anyway. She'd avoided a potentially disastrous situation and so had he.

She should be concentrating on helping him professionally, she decided, by bringing more attention to the need for this trial. Who didn't want a role model like Franco? she thought. Someone strong, who fought for love and health and prosperity…and adventures. She was still overwhelmed that she'd been riding a Vespa with no accidents all this time.

Franco was an audacious explorer in many

ways, and she was already learning more from him than she'd thought she would. Now the idea that had struck her at the castle kept growing from a spark into a furious fire inside her, flooding her with a sense of purpose she hadn't felt in years.

CHAPTER EIGHT

FRANCO HAD BEEN on call since six a.m. with barely a break, and now he was looking at a screen displaying a portly thirty-nine-year-old man's insides. Beside him sat Adrienne, one of her long legs crossed elegantly over the other. But there was a rather large elephant lumbering around in the room with them. It had been hovering there ever since he'd left her on her bike earlier in the week, and not even the diagnosis they were about to give could make it fully disappear.

'Your MRI results have revealed a small spasm in your lower colon, but the colonoscopy, as you know, could not be completed. The surgeon had trouble getting the scope past an unusual lesion…'

'Yes, I felt that, thank you.'

Their patient, a Greek man named Diodoro, tapped his feet anxiously on the floor tiles. He wore too-white sneakers, and his plump arms shook with the movements, sending ripples through his belly.

The man's partner, a slightly slimmer Italian-Asian in a green V-neck sweater and fashionably mismatched socks, put a hand to his shoulder. 'You felt it? I thought you were sedated?'

'Obviously not sedated enough, Gabriel.'

Franco watched Adrienne wait patiently, and then continue unperturbed. She was always so poised, he thought—until she let her guard down. That night when she'd started to open up about her life—the real, personal side of it—he'd seen the Adrienne he wanted to see more of. But then she'd clammed up again.

Just for a moment she'd looked like a wilting flower, running out of water, but he was still none the wiser about her past. There was something that had pushed her to come here aside from wanting her oncology rotation. But she wasn't about to divulge any personal details beyond those he needed to know—that much was clear. He'd wondered if maybe there *was* a guy she was being urged to marry…and that was what had ended her other relationship.

No, he thought now, catching her eyes on him again. There was no one, as she'd said. Not with the way she'd started to look at *him*…

He could have kissed her the other night. He'd felt the build-up, experienced a wave of lust he'd never felt before—and not just because she was so untouchable. Well, maybe not entirely untouchable, he thought. She hadn't dropped his hand when he'd taken it at the castle, and the thought of introducing her to a decidedly un-royal world of pleasure had made its way into his dreams on several hot, restless occasions this past week.

There was also the fact that women were usually intimidated by his wealth and his status in society. But Adrienne wasn't. She would always be the one people wanted to talk to, in any room. Part of him admired that—even if her status wasn't exactly her choice.

Knowing Ivan was always around, protecting her, made him burn even harder to get her alone, but there wasn't much point in letting this go any further anyway. She was the future Queen of Lisri, for God's sake. It was better this way…staying at a safe, professional distance. Better not to let that feeling in his heart rattle loose, nor allow himself this unsettling sense of dependence on seeing her and having her close.

Not if she ends up being someone else you might lose.

'So, we've looked at your CT pneumocolon… that's a virtual colonoscopy…and the results from your biopsy, and we can now tell you we've found something,' Adrienne was saying now.

She glanced his way and Franco bowed his head. This was always the worst part. Every doctor was trained to deliver bad news, but when it came to cancer it was still not the done thing to mention the C word outright. In saying they'd found *something*, Adrienne was leaving it up to the patient to come to his own conclusions and mention it first.

'It's cancer. Right, Doctors?' Diodoro wasn't beating around the bush.

'Yes, I'm afraid it is,' Adrienne confirmed.

'It's a death sentence, isn't it?' He wrung his hands in his lap, ran them over his dark denim jeans, then stood up, and Franco watched his shoulders fall with every step towards the window.

'Don't be ridiculous, Dio. You're always so dramatic.' Gabriel crossed one leg over the other, maybe trying to disguise his portly belly.

Diodoro turned, his face reddening. 'A lot of people just saw me hugging my knees with a tube up my butt, Gabriel. Am I not allowed to be a little dramatic?'

'Oh, honey, I've seen you do worse things,' his partner quipped, deadpan.

To Franco's surprise, Diodoro erupted into laughter, but when Gabriel got up and embraced him hard all laughter stopped, and both men fell silent in their trembling embrace.

'We'll get through this,' Gabriel whispered.

'It's not necessarily a death sentence. Fortunately, we've caught it early,' Adrienne went on.

Franco pushed the patient file closer to her, brushing the tips of her fingernails. 'When you're comfortable we can bring the surgeon in, and we'll discuss the details,' he said.

Diodoro nodded, sinking down into the couch again, apparently in shock. Franco felt for the man; it was impossible not to become personally invested in his patients—on some level, at least. Meeting the woman with Ewing's would be tough, but at least he'd be more prepared now...if his damn phone calls would ever get answered.

They needed just a few more weeks, the authorities kept saying.

Just a few more weeks to feed them the same old line about needing just a few more weeks, he thought.

Adrienne was walking their patient through the highlights of a new treatment—one that the Perretta Institute had helped bring out of trial and into general use. It was a revolutionary radiation technique that they would try prior to surgery—with the patient's consent. It had been a huge success so far, and just last week had sent two similar cases into remission in Rome.

When Franco took over, explaining what he knew, Adrienne took copious notes on her clipboard. She was so invested in the institute already. He knew she remembered almost everything she heard and read. He'd caught her poring over some of the documents she'd asked for a couple of days back, reading up on the patients on the Ewing's trial, the achievements and results they'd seen before it had all got held up. She was doing him proud and they were a good match in lots of ways.

But every now and then, watching her lips move, he wondered what might have happened that night if he *had* made the first move on the princess.

Diodoro's substantial mouth was compressed into a thin, grim line. 'Butt surgery. Who'd have thought it would come to this? By a princess, too.'

Franco bit his cheek, hiding a smile in his paperwork.

Adrienne drew a deep breath. 'I'm not a surgeon,' she said, 'but I can be present for any procedures if you want me to be.'

'I will indeed think about that. I'm grateful for your work here, Dr Princess,' Diodoro replied humbly.

'Dr Balthus is fine.'

Franco spotted Adrienne in the staff canteen later. She seemed to be engrossed in another research paper, alone at a table in the corner, until surgeon Ansell Ackerman made a move for her table.

Franco rolled his eyes and considered going over there himself, but she stood up abruptly and left to take a call, sweeping right past Ansell distractedly, without acknowledging him. Franco swore he heard her say something about the cat.

Ansell sloped dejectedly back to another table,

which wasn't the way he usually exited a situation in this place.

But there was no time to waste on empty victories. Franco barely had time to grab a sandwich, as their Ewing's sarcoma patient, Rosita, would be here soon with her parents, and it was almost time for him to face some personal demons. It would be difficult, and painful, but Adrienne hadn't been afraid to tell him the truth. Ewing's sarcoma patients were rare, and he would never be fully ready to face one, but he was still always going to be the best person in the room.

He was frustrated beyond belief that phase three of the trial was still blocked at all angles. Still, Adrienne's determined words at the castle about her helping him get it through had stuck with him—as had the look in her eyes when they'd each silently dared the other to close the damn deal and kiss, regardless of any consequences.

'I just keep telling myself that this can't be right... she's only twenty-four years old.'

Mr Vettraino, Rosita's father, was in the denial stage. His well-cut navy double-breasted jacket, jeans and polished shoes reminded Franco of his brother.

'There must be something we can do.'

'That's why we're here,' Franco said kindly.

He'd prepared himself, reading late into the

night, and before that chasing down more blocked avenues. He couldn't mention the trial now and get anyone's hopes up, and Adrienne knew it. But he would do the best he could.

The look on Rosita's face every time her father gave in to his emotions tore at his heart. Rosita was too thin already, with sad brown eyes and black hair in a slicked-back ponytail. She was turning her phone around in her hands, staring unseeingly at the leaflets and forms on the table.

'We know you have experience with patients who've developed this…this cancer,' her mother said. The prim-looking woman toyed with the top button of her pinstriped blouse and sat forward in her seat, making the pearls in her golden hoop earrings catch the sun. 'We're all so very grateful you're with us on this, Doctor. And you, Dr Balthus,' she added. 'Your work gives me hope. We'll do anything. Anything she needs.'

'The survival rate for localised Ewing's sarcoma is significantly higher than it was several years ago,' he explained, noticing that the woman's wedding ring—a thin gold band—was next to a not-so-modest-sized diamond. 'That's pretty high. But there are new treatments on the way, and we've caught it early. We do have options here.'

Adrienne pushed a box of tissues towards them and caught his eye. He knew they both wished they could talk about the success they'd seen in phase two of the new treatment. There was a young woman's future at stake—the future of a woman who should have the world at her feet, not a hospital floor.

'Now, Rosita, you're entitled to some help—and not just here at the hospital.' Adrienne's voice was warm, her manner well-honed. 'You'll have occupational therapy, palliative care and community nursing support. And we'll be here with you every step of the way.'

As Adrienne went on he watched the rise and fall of Rosita's emotions in her eyes and wondered what it would be like to have a daughter. He'd proposed to Luci with a ring not unlike the one on Mrs Vettraino's finger—big, lavish, with a diamond so sparkly it had sent rainbows across every white wall when the sun hit it. But Luci hadn't wanted children. Funny how he'd just accepted that, no question, without really thinking about if he wanted them himself. Maybe he would have considered it down the line. But he knew Luci would never have changed her mind. She'd been adamant.

For the first time he wondered if maybe... just maybe...they *wouldn't* have lasted for ever. They'd been so young, after all, and they'd both dived headfirst into a serious relationship. He didn't know many people who'd got together that young and still wanted the same things from each other years later.

He doted on his niece, Alina, only marginally less than her father, Benni, did—he had never missed a single one of her gymnastics competitions. Alina was eight years old now, with rosy cheeks, inquisitive round green eyes and a head of chestnut curls.

He and his family had become so much closer after Luci died. He often thought her death had hammered home the importance of not sweating the small stuff, of talking things through and never going to bed angry with anyone or leaving anything important unsaid. He felt better for clearing things up with Adrienne over why he'd missed that first consult with Rosita, even if it had left things between them even more perplexing.

'How long before I die if no treatment works?' Rosita's voice was cool when she spoke, composed.

Her mother drew a sharp breath and snatched a tissue from the box. 'Don't ask things like that.'

'Why, Mamma? I want to know. It's my body, and I have a right to know how long it will be mine for. Will I lose the ability to walk eventually? Who will walk Bones?'

'You've called your dog Bones?' Franco asked her, and she nodded at her shoes.

'He's nine. If he dies before me, I guess at least he'll meet me up there.' She raised her eyes to the ceiling and jabbed at the air with her phone.

Her father took the seat beside her, exhaling deeply. 'She keeps talking like this, Doctors.' Then he turned to his daughter, revealing a hint of a gold chain under his white-collared shirt. 'I told you…this man can help you.'

'We will *all* do what we can,' Adrienne said.

'It's a rare but curable cancer if it's caught in time,' Franco told them, feeling Adrienne's eyes on him. She was clearly trying to take the pressure off him and it made him start for a second. Was she concerned that he might fall apart or something?

'Will she require chemo?' Rosita's mother grabbed for another tissue. 'Won't that just put her off her food? She's already lost so much weight—look at her.'

Rosita shot Franco a look that included an eye-roll. She was acting defiant, but she was probably back to being stomped on by that raging bull of bad news whenever she was alone. He knew it well.

Adrienne explained how a nine-week chemo course prior to surgery or radiation would help reduce the size of the tumour, and he focused on her calm, lilting voice, summoning strength by osmosis.

He knew the chemo drug they *weren't* talking about—the one on the trial—might possibly help Rosita faster. It would potentially cut the number of cycles in half…maybe even less. It would mean less pain for her, more time for doing regular things, like walking in parks, chatting to people online...maybe about her cancer? He wondered who she'd talk to about this. Luci had often complained that no one knew how she was feeling, and how could he have disagreed?

Back then, if he'd known about any treatment that might have saved Luci even an ounce of her pain, and someone had been keeping it under lock and key for no good reason...he didn't like to think what he might have done.

'I wish we could have told them about the trial. Any news on that? You didn't mention it, so I'm guessing not.'

Adrienne closed the door after the family, leaving them alone.

'Not yet,' he said, pacing to the window.

His brain was still whirring over all the questions they'd answered, and how he'd talked briefly about Luci when Rosita's father had brought up a child they'd read about who'd been treated in Rome. It hadn't been as bad as he'd expected. He had more hope for the future these days, and there was a new fire under his backside making him want to do even more.

'I offered to help, remember? And I have had a few ideas, actually.'

'I'm handling it—although I'm still waiting

on the authorities,' he said distractedly. 'But I'll keep that in mind, thank you.'

He knew she could probably use her name to open a few doors, and he'd take her up on that if it came to it, but he owed it to his team to do everything he could personally regarding the issue before pulling a student into it—and that was what Adrienne was, after all, her royal status notwithstanding.

'Did I hear you say something about your cat?' he remembered suddenly as she pulled her phone out.

'She's gone missing.' She frowned into her screen, resting on the edge of the desk, revealing several more inches of smooth pale leg under her white coat. 'Mirabel the housekeeper hasn't seen her today, and she usually comes in for food.'

'Maybe everyone else is feeding her too?' he offered, but she shook her head.

'She never goes far from my apartment. I'm sure she's fine, but…'

'Go home,' he said, but she shook her head again.

'Don't be silly. I'm too busy.'

'Go,' he insisted. 'There's only an hour left of your shift. I'll tell one of the nurses to cover your last round.'

She offered him a thankful *namaste* hand sign and hurried out of the room. Then she stuck her

head back in. 'Are you OK?' she asked. 'After...
that?'

The question struck him deep. A missing cat
on her mind and she was remembering to check
in on *him*. And she'd already seen that he wasn't
fine, mostly due to his frustration over all these
vexing trial setbacks.

He told her yes, and motioned for her to hurry,
then followed her, catching sight of her shrug-
ging out of her white coat and swinging through
the double doors.

Nothing would have happened to the cat. He
was pretty sure of that. But he knew by now that
Adrienne's cool exterior was all an act. She cared
deeply about lots of things; she just didn't always
talk about them with him. Who *did* she talk to?

She must really love that cat, he thought, hoping nothing *had* happened to it.

CHAPTER NINE

MR GEORDANO, HER oropharyngeal cancer patient, who had at first treated her royal presence with such disdain, had sent flowers again via the hospital. He was thanking her like this every few days now. She'd taken them home, and the scent of wild roses almost overpowered her the second she stepped inside.

'Puss?'

'She still hasn't been here,' said Mirabel, poking her head out from the kitchen holding a scouring pad and making her jump.

Adrienne tossed her bag to the couch, shook off her shoes and hurried the length of the apartment.

Panic was setting in now. Fiamma was the closest thing she had to a friend around here; she couldn't let her down.

In less than five minutes she'd sent Ivan off one way, despite his initial reluctance, and sped off the other way on her own.

As she headed south along the coast towards Solerno, the city soon fell into a backdrop. Looming mountains up ahead confirmed she was well out of her comfort zone. But she was not to be deterred. Upping her speed on the Vespa, all she could think about was Fiamma.

What if something was terribly wrong? What if she never saw the kitten again? The cat was the only one who knew all her secrets.

'Puss!' she called out, and felt her scarf blow from around her neck, right into the branches of a tree. Damn. She couldn't stop and go back for it. What if Fiamma was out here somewhere, looking for her, lost?

But could she have wandered this far?

Pulling to a stop on a grassy patch, Adrienne left the engine on, checked her map again. The arrow was all over the place, telling her to ride into the ocean.

'Thanks a lot,' she grumbled at it, flipping the bike's stand down and cutting the engine. She shook her phone. As if in defiance the battery sign turned ominously red. Ten per cent left. *Great.*

Flustered and hot, and apparently in the middle of nowhere, between villages on a narrow coastal road, she turned the bike around carefully. It stuttered beneath her, hot and tired like she was, from a thirty-five-minute bakeathon in the sun.

'Don't you give up on me,' she ordered it, speeding back the way she'd come.

The road was beautiful. She tried to let the view relax her. It was all trees and wildflowers springing from mossy curves and corners. But she was still on edge after her work today, and the missing kitten was an added worry on top.

Franco was concerned that the trial would not be ready for Rosita in time. He wanted to try the new drug before she had too many cycles of regular chemo.

It sounded as if he didn't want her help in bypassing all the bureaucratic barriers—but that, unbeknown to him, was her speciality. She didn't just smile and shake hands with people in her royal life. Maybe he wanted to handle it on his own, like he'd handled things so far, without the help of a royal name—he was a proud Italian after all.

She hadn't told him about her idea yet. Instead, she'd confided in her mother the Queen about it in a letter, hoping that maybe she'd ignite a spark of excitement over something of such importance.

It had poured out of her so effortlessly—how a new website and app she had in mind would offer a network of support to cancer patients and survivors. How she already had an interview lined up with a young girl Bianca, now in her early twenties, who'd been in remission for over three years, thanks to having the new chemo drug when it was on trial. The drugs that were now being blocked from reaching more people. It wouldn't be so hard to find more interviews and get the word out…

I'm excited to have your support on this. I'm confident I can be someone who will in time help build a solid foundation for the health and prosperity of our country and beyond.

She'd also written about Franco, and the lives he was shaping and mostly saving, and how she felt useful now, but wanted to do even more.

Every time she'd written his name she'd felt her stomach bottom out, but she'd not mentioned her growing affections, just her work. *Their* work.

She had made no mention of Baron Vittorio La Rosa. Hopefully her mother would get the hint that she wasn't interested in him. But she *had* tried to be encouraging about her baking.

It's never too late to do something different, Mother, even something no one expects of a royal.

No reply to her letter had arrived yet. No phone call either. That was a little disconcerting…

Just then a motorcycle appeared from nowhere. It shot past her on the bend so fast she panicked, then shrieked and hit the brakes.

Everything happened in a blur. Skidding. Hot pain. The Vespa tumbling over the cliff edge. The next thing she registered was that she was flat on her back, grass bunched in her tight fists, and her right leg was burning like fire.

She staggered to the rocky precipice and peered down at the Vespa, clutching her arm. Her burnt ankle was sore, but she'd been lucky. *Very* lucky. The bike was now in pieces and smoking threateningly. Somewhere down there, she assumed, was her phone, gone to join it.

Lowering herself carefully beneath a tree, she studied her injuries. She would have a bloody and bruised ankle for a while, but she could walk. She turned her ankle, testing it, and winced, then tore the bottom off her shirt to make a bandage. It hurt like hell when she yanked it tight.

The road both ways was empty. But it was too hot to get back out into the sun. And what if someone else who felt like killing her came around the corner? The motorcyclist hadn't even stopped—what was wrong with some people?

Someone would find her, she told herself, and her shock was wearing off. But it wasn't safe, being out here alone like this. Hadn't someone said mountain lions lived out here? Or was that something else she'd imagined?

It felt as if hours had passed as she looked out for lions, waiting for someone—anyone—to come along. The sun gleamed its golden hues across the moss, like it did in Lisri an hour before their famous sunsets.

What would her mother say if she could see her now? She could never find out that this had happened, Adrienne decided. Papa would say her being alone again was not an option, like he always did. He'd probably remove Ivan, citing him as unsuitable, and send for a team of bodyguards to go with her everywhere.

She was just about to resign herself to limping down the road in search of assistance when another motorbike tore into view. She knew that bike.

'Franco?'

The strength she'd been summoning melted away as Franco almost skidded on his own bike in his rush to get to her. 'Adrienne!'

She tried to move away from the tree to meet him. It still felt too long until he reached her, and she held back a sob as he half fell to the ground beside her. Maybe she was in more shock than she'd thought.

'What happened? Stay still.' He crouched over her, deep concern etched around his eyes, his bare knees pressed into the scratchy grass. He started examining her leg and the gash across her arm, while she insisted she was fine.

'Where's the bike?' he asked. She motioned to the cliff-edge, wincing as she tried to move her foot again.

'Keep it still. You did a good job with the bandage… Can you walk?'

'Yes.'

His hand felt cool and soothing on her bruises. And his touch…dear God, his touch…

Her scarf was sticking out from under his bike seat. He must have seen it in the branches of that tree.

He shuffled to the cliff edge quickly. He seemed to take in the sight for less than a second before striding back to her, shoulders tensed, fists clenched, every muscle strained.

'I'm so sorry, Franco, but I had to swerve to miss another bike. Then this happened.'

His jaw ticked as his shadow consumed her. 'I don't care about the bike. It could have been you down there.'

He helped her up onto her one good foot, looping his arm around her waist and mostly carrying her as she attempted to hobble to his bike.

'I called your phone, but it's dead. I had a feeling you'd be out looking for the kitten and I was worried. You don't know these roads well enough.'

'I do now.'

'This is serious.'

His voice was gruff as he hoisted her up into his arms and paused with his face an inch away from hers. She told him she was sorry again as she searched his eyes. His pupils seemed to be dilated with repressed rage and something else... He cared about her more than he was letting on. The sudden recognition made her feel hot and weak all at once.

'Something really bad could have happened

to you, Adrienne. You're probably in shock. I'm taking you to the hospital.'

'No,' she said, panic stabbing at her core.

He lowered her carefully onto the bike. The sun was sinking behind him now, and he gently placed her helmet back over her head, clasped it shut with purpose.

'No,' she said again as he mounted the seat in front of her. She clutched his shirt urgently and his muscles tensed, his back rigid as a wall. 'No hospital. Promise me.'

He turned on the engine and pulled onto the road slowly, carefully, so as not to hurt her any more. 'Why no hospital?'

'I can't have anyone knowing what happened and it would get out. Someone always talks. It would be awful, and ultimately unhelpful. And I'm completely fine, I promise.'

'You don't look fine to me. Where the hell is Ivan?'

'I sent him to look the other way. It's just a few bruises. Please, Franco, if you take me anywhere, take me home.'

She could hear her own voice trembling and felt his shoulders slacken.

'You're impossible,' he huffed, and she breathed a sigh of relief. She knew she could trust him.

But he didn't say another word the whole ride back.

CHAPTER TEN

A SHORT, ROUND woman in an apron stopped her vacuum cleaner abruptly when he stepped through the doorway.

'We need to get her lying down. I have to look at her.'

He helped Adrienne down the hall, using his right side as a crutch. The housekeeper fussed around them and cleared the path, then assembled a cushiony pillow at one end of a plush aubergine-coloured sofa. The sofa faced doors wide open to the sky, and the Gulf of Naples with all its stars. It was an impressive space.

'Mirabel, I'm fine…it's nothing,' Adrienne protested as he slid her shoes off and dropped them to the polished hardwood floor.

His heart was still high on adrenaline. He'd had a sudden feeling of dread that she'd gone out looking for the kitten instead of sending her staff, so he'd left an hour after her and taken three different routes before he'd seen her scarf.

She should be at the hospital now. He'd almost turned around several times to take her there for an X-ray. But…damn stubborn woman that she was…she'd trusted him not to do that.

'Where's your first aid bag?' he asked, and she directed him to the kitchen.

The apartment was too big for one person, with huge appliances, a bigger fridge than his, and a dining table behind the sofa that would seat ten people. The views were truly fit for a princess.

She probably had a really good view of Vesuvius from the bedrooms upstairs, he thought idly as he located her first aid kit, but he wasn't taking her anywhere else with injuries like this—and definitely not with the housekeeper here.

Her ankle wasn't quite as bad as it had looked once he'd cleaned the grit out—and she could walk, thank God. She proved it when a soft meow from the balcony sent her leaping from the couch.

'Fiamma?'

He caught her, and Mirabel went for the kitten, scooping the small grey thing up in her arms.

'She came back! Oh, Mirabel, give her to me, please.'

Adrienne let him help her back to the couch, and he watched her press the kitten's furry grey head to her cheek. The kitten snuggled in for a moment, then sprang away to explore the rug around the gilded glass coffee table.

'That creature has no idea what you just went through,' he said crossly, and then bit his tongue. The sight of her on the road, and seeing that bike in pieces over the edge… It could have been *her* taking a cliff dive.

Mirabel was watching them, scrutinising him as he massaged Adrienne's leg from where he crouched on the floor in front of her.

Adrienne reached for her housekeeper's hand, drawing her in. 'Don't say anything about this to my parents, Mirabel.'

Mirabel looked uncomfortable. 'Does he have an appointment…? To be here…?'

'Of course he doesn't have an *appointment*, Mirabel. He just scraped me off the side of a road.' She paused, visibly regaining her composure. 'Don't say anything about any of this. I expect this to stay private—do you understand?'

Franco watched Adrienne jerk her gaze to him and back again, and took the hint and made his exit out to the balcony. The cat sprang after him and he watched it leap at shadows around the plant pots, trying not to listen to her and the housekeeper. She was trying to keep *him* a secret as much as her accident, and that grated on his nerves.

He'd noticed on the way in that someone had sent her flowers. The gift card was still sticking out of the bouquet. She probably had admirers everywhere. How many men had made it up here? Or was he really the first?

The door had closed after Mirabel and now Franco sat cross-legged on the soft rug. There was no way he was leaving her yet. His calls could wait. He didn't ask about her family—she'd panicked about them enough tonight—but he did ask if she needed anything, and she said that she needed stories to take her mind off everything that had happened.

'I like your stories,' she told him, settling back on the pillows on the sofa. 'You tell them with such passion, Franco. Anyone who's ever done anything great has been passionate about it, driven by it. Obsessed with it. Your passion was the first thing I noticed about you.'

'Is that right?'

Watching her lips singing his praises was intoxicating, as much as her penchant for secrecy was frustrating. He dared to reach a hand to her face, swept a strand of soft hair back behind her ear and let it linger as she scanned his eyes. He couldn't recall ever telling her a story with the passion she found so striking, but maybe she just liked the way he talked. Right now, he realised he was probably what Benni would call 'a sucker', but he knew he'd do anything the so-called Ice Princess asked.

So he told her of the legends surrounding the islands, of slayers and fighters and a fire-breathing dragon. He told her about the ghost he'd once seen in the catacombs, and how he'd befriended a pod of dolphins who had sailed with him to Capri in the wake of his yacht.

He'd thought she might get tired, but she kept

her blue eyes on him, transfixed, till it took every atom of his self-restraint not to kiss her. What he really wanted to say was still repressed, like a dragon in a cave inside his chest. He hated leaving it to fester inside him…

Everything in his right mind told him to get up and leave her, but she was hurt, dammit. And stubborn.

CHAPTER ELEVEN

ADRIENNE HAD WANDERED out to the balcony, testing her ankle. It felt a lot better already, and Franco had had every excuse to leave her over the past couple of hours, but he hadn't. He'd kept her mind off reality, as she'd asked him to, but she felt his presence behind her in the doorway now, watching her like a falcon. It was strange and exciting, having him here, but if Mirabel told anyone…

'What the hell were you thinking—seriously?'

His voice made her stomach reassemble itself on the spot. She turned to him.

'I don't even think you understand the severity of what you just did—taking that bike out there on those roads, on your own. With or without a speeding bike coming at you, you don't know this place, how to handle those roads. You could be lying dead at the bottom of a cliff!'

She stared at him, shocked. She'd never heard him raise his voice, but she knew it meant he cared. She could see it—just as she had when she'd been collapsed at the side of the road—like a fire burning in his eyes, almost out of control.

'I've already told you I'm sorry.' Her mouth was dry.

'You have no idea, do you? What you're doing to me?'

His words struck her like a lightning bolt and his eyes tore through her weak apology to the very core of her. They both knew what they were doing to each other—what they'd been denying for weeks. The realisation left her aching to reach for him, but he huffed and looked out at the expanse of sea on the horizon, as if composing himself.

She hugged her arms around herself. 'Listen, Franco. Whatever this is…'

She couldn't finish her sentence. As if magnetised by some invisible force, Franco strode to her from the doorway and a second later her arms had taken over, reaching for him so she could lose herself in his urgent, passionate kisses.

Her hands found themselves pulling at his shirt blindly and her lips fused to his as he walked them backwards, conscious all the time of her injured leg and her arm. Each kiss slowed into a sensuous new discovery, then sped up into another frenzied exploration until somehow they were back on the couch.

After weeks of waiting she felt sharp shocks of fire and lightning tear through her legs, her womb and her belly. She could barely breathe as he claimed her tongue in hot, delicious swirls, slowing down and speeding up like a song she instinctively knew how to dance to. They were chest to chest, hips to hips, in a cloud of cushions, and her whole world in that moment consisted of just his mouth, his lips and hands, and the places they took her to. She had never been kissed like this before.

'We should stop,' she heard herself saying suddenly. What the hell was she doing, giving in to this glorious, unrestrained, *frightening* passion?

Even as he uncoiled his limbs from hers, she bunched the fabric of his shirt in both her hands. She knew she had to let him go, but her body couldn't do it.

Franco slid from her grasp to the floor, ran his hands through his crop of messed-up hair and blinked at the room as if he'd been pulled out of a dream much too quickly. Her heart was on fire, her face still stinging with the friction from his stubbled jaw.

Reckless, reckless woman.

That heavenly place they'd just gone to together was exactly where she'd feared she'd end up if they got any closer. Her lips throbbed, wanting more of him. She sat up, grateful for the sea breeze blowing through the doors, and felt her breaths come hot and heavy as she forced herself up on shaky legs and walked past him to the kitchen.

'We didn't hurt your ankle, did we?' she heard him say eventually, his voice raspy like hers.

She wasn't even thinking about her injuries now. Dazed, she filled a glass with cold water and drank it thirstily, then pressed her hands to the counter, eyes closed, still tasting him, wanting more. So much more.

He stepped up behind her, dwarfing her in his shadow. 'I'm sorry,' he whispered gruffly, and she squeezed her eyes closed.

She wished he didn't have to be sorry. She wished he hadn't had to hear her telling Mirabel not to mention him being here. She wanted him here more than anything—surely he knew that. But just because she was being paranoid it didn't mean her family might not still try to stop her completing the fellowship, and warn Franco away from her if they found out her boss had been here in her apartment, tending to her wounds as a result of lending her a dangerous vehicle himself.

'That shouldn't have happened,' she forced herself to say. Because it wouldn't end well for him. It was stupid and selfish of her, at the end of the day.

He gently pressed his lips to the back of her neck, let his kisses rain along her skin, leaving a trail of tingles. She shivered involuntarily, surrendering momentarily to his worship, and he turned her around, took the glass from her. His eyes locked onto hers and his carnal desire churned up the air between them like a Catherine wheel.

He exhaled, saying her name again, and ran a thumb across the hollow beneath her left cheekbone. An electric thrill threatened to make her knees buckle. The gesture, and the desire in his eyes, resonated through every fibre of her being.

'I shouldn't have kissed you.' He drew her closer by the nape of her neck, and she closed her eyes despite herself. 'But, for the record, I do want to kiss you again, Princess Adrienne.'

'Don't call me that,' she groaned, pressing her forehead to his chest over his heart.

He broke away and turned away to the counter beside her. Instantly, she wanted his protective cocoon back.

His deep green gaze cut into her and he laughed without smiling. 'You are who you are, Adrienne. You're a member of a royal family. Why would you want to forget that? Don't you want to be a ruler for Lisri?'

She pulled out a chair at the dining table and dropped into it, needing to create some kind of distance between them as well as to have something stable beneath her unsteady feet. Her ankle was starting to throb again—all her fault...they'd got carried away.

'Of course I do. But it means this thing between us can't ever go anywhere.'

The words coming out of her mouth felt so

wrong. The thought of going further, having his hand, his mouth, on her breasts and between her thighs, touching her and stretching out the night with endless incredible wanton sex, made her fold her arms weakly on the table and put her head down, as if blocking him from view might make the whole thing go away.

It was imperative now that she should warn him off, tell him why it wasn't wise for either of them to go down this road. Except they'd only had one kiss; he would think she was crazy, surely.

Her world was different from his. A kiss like that, and a heart like hers…it would be impossible for her not to keep on falling for him from this point forward. It might even turn into love on her side. But she'd be broken apart all over again when it ended. And so might he.

'It just can't happen again,' she affirmed. 'I mean it.'

He was too far away, even only at the other end of the table. Then he went and gathered up his bike helmet and jacket, sending a crashing agony right through her. She watched him shrug the muscled arms that had just been wrapped around her into the leather sleeves and knew she wouldn't rest unless she told him the truth.

'You're so different from him…you're everything he wasn't.'

'Prince Xavier?' Franco's eyes darkened.

'Xavier was cheating on me. That's the truth,

Franco. I never told anyone, and no one else knows except my parents. So I couldn't marry him. But he's a royal, you see, like me. That's what they want most of all—a merger of two noble families.'

Franco processed her words in silence as she told him everything—what had happened the night the engagement was meant to be announced, how her father had still insisted Xavier was a good match because of his lineage, how the press had twisted everything, thanks to Xavier's lies. Holding his helmet under one arm, he studied her face and for once she couldn't read him.

'I'm sorry for what you went through,' he said after a moment. 'I have no desire to be "noble", if that's how your family defines it,' he added gruffly.

She swallowed. Of course he didn't want to be the next Prince Consort of Lisri. What she'd just told him would have scared him off for life, even if he wasn't still devoted to his dead fiancée. She fixed her aching head high, feeling the emotions inside her crashing harder than the real collision.

'They want me to marry some *baron* now,' she added for good measure. 'I haven't even met him myself. But if it's not him, it'll be someone else. They know, because I've told them often enough, that I'll only marry for love, but they will keep on lining them up…'

'Well, that's that, then, isn't it?' he said, studying her eyes again. 'We could sit here all night finding more reasons why that kiss shouldn't have happened, Adrienne. Or we could just leave it here.'

She couldn't tell if he was hurt, angry, or both.

Her insides were screaming. For a second she almost succumbed to her urge to pull him back to her, but he tugged the zip of his jacket up to his neck, and she pursed her still-stinging lips. God, she wanted to grab him again and not let go. He would probably never kiss her again now— ever—but it was for the best if he didn't. For both of them.

'Sleep on the couch,' he instructed from the doorway, back to being a doctor in a heartbeat. 'Don't try going upstairs. I'll come and check on you in the morning. Do I need an appointment?'

'No,' she managed.

'Do you need me to stay to make sure you're OK? I can carry you up to your room and I'll sleep on the couch.'

His question seemed to float around the chandelier, and she flashed her eyes back to the couch again, swallowing hard. She would never look at it the same way after tonight. 'I'll be perfectly fine, thank you.'

He lowered his head, as if biting back more words that would do neither of them any good. Then he left before she had the chance to change her mind.

CHAPTER TWELVE

FRANCO WAS FIVE minutes late. When he knocked on the door, Adrienne and Stefano, a radiation oncologist, were already present with Diodoro Merten.

Adrienne looked up as he walked in, and Franco swore he saw her cheeks redden slightly, though she was careful not to meet his eyes. Four days since their kiss, he thought, counting backwards in his head. And she'd been very careful to avoid being alone with him ever since.

Good. You don't need that drama in your life.

They were meeting briefly, prior to Mr Merten's first radiation treatment. Adrienne was explaining again how they'd seen some great success with it, and he took a seat behind the desk, explaining, when and where he could, the clear trend towards it in the colorectal cancer community worldwide, and this new treatment's ability to increase both pathological and clinical remission rates.

To anyone else in the room he was quite sure they seemed like nothing but professionals and colleagues, but their secret burned beneath every word they spoke to each other.

He'd kept himself busy away from her. He'd

been through enough heartache for a lifetime with Luci—there was no way he was going there again, or putting his affairs in the spotlight, to be raked through like garbage by the media.

That bastard Xavier had come off almost saint-like and unscathed after what he'd done to her, and here was Adrienne, still expected to marry the next aristocratic idiot her family saw fit to pawn her off on. If that was what being a royal was like—no thanks. He wanted no part of it. Though he had also been thinking a lot about how strong she was—probably more than she gave herself credit for—pulling herself back together after all that nonsense and refocusing on her goals and career.

'Knock-knock!' Gabriel, Diodoro's partner, swept into the room, carrying a large coffee. 'Sorry! I had to beat the damn machine to get milk into this thing, and let me tell you it wasn't worth it. Where do you get your milk from? Pangolins? Otters?'

'Oats, actually,' Adrienne said as Gabriel took a seat. 'It can take some getting used to.'

'What happened to your ankle, Doctor?' Gabriel asked, gesturing to her bandage.

Franco busied himself with the CT scans and treatment plan in front of him as she said something vague about coming off her bike. Had she told anyone the truth? he wondered. Had that housekeeper said anything about him being there without a damned appointment? Or asked her why he, specifically, had come to find her?

'Sounds like you got lucky,' Diodoro told her, frowning.

'Can't say as much for the bike,' Franco cut in, looking up from his paperwork.

Adrienne looked thoroughly embarrassed for a second. He regretted the dig almost instantly. He couldn't care less about the bike and neither could Aimee. It could be easily replaced. Adrienne couldn't. He was just on edge. Unsettled by the fact that she'd been on his mind since she'd called him the next morning, insisted her foot was fine and that he shouldn't come to the apartment to check on her.

He should be glad that his heart had been given a get-out clause. He wasn't a blueblood like her, for a start, and she wasn't free to love who she wanted to love—she'd said so herself. Some law would have her marrying the next suitable aristocrat, even if she *was* waiting for love. Why mess with a royal court pre-programmed to keep him away? Why get his heart all torn up? Again.

Forget her kiss…her addictive taste.

Forget those imploring eyes.

Forget it all.

Diodoro and Gabriel were laughing at something now, albeit nervously. Franco had zoned out, but Adrienne seemed to be doing a good job of warming them up prior to the first treatment session. He heard her tell them how impressed she was by their support for each other during this time. Ever the romantic, he thought, wishing he didn't have so much in common with the bits of her heart he'd been entrusted to see.

'I just love how he loves me, Dr Princess Balthus,' Diodoro said, laying his head on Gabriel's bony shoulder. 'He makes me laugh, and he listens to my soul. I think, when you find that with someone, you have the best thing this world has to offer.'

He exhaled deeply as Gabriel dropped a kiss on the top of his balding head. 'You big softie,' Gabriel said, and smiled.

Franco felt the same envy he saw in Adrienne's eyes.

'At least, I used to think that,' Diodoro continued despondently. 'Now I know good health is more important.'

When they'd left the room, the space was filled with the sound of Franco's buzzing phone.

'Hey, Dad.'

Marco Perretta asked after Adrienne, which made a ball of knots in his stomach. 'Yeah, she's here. But…'

Adrienne looked at him curiously, one hand on the doorknob. Trust his father to ask to see her now. He wouldn't wait for anyone—not even a princess.

* * *

Down in the busy entrance hall, his father stopped his low whisper of a phone conversation to address them both properly. Dressed in his trademark purple tie and his best suit, he looked ready to stand up in court—but then Marco Perretta always dressed ready for an occasion.

Adrienne smiled politely throughout his introduction to his father, and Franco wondered briefly what it would be like to meet *her* father, Alexander Marx-Balthus, Prince Consort of Lisri. It would probably be in some castle, or a private room draped in gold-plated accolades and tributes. Not that he would ever get to meet her family. His blood might be a rare AB negative, but it was still not pure enough for them, he thought bitterly.

'My daughter happened to mention there was some sort of misplacement issue with a bike you borrowed.'

Marco led them both outside into the bright morning sunlight, which sent white streaks through his thick greying hair and made Franco wonder, as he always did, whether his hair would end up the same way.

'I've had Benni arrange a new bike. Same model. Where should I have it sent? Maybe to your place, son?'

'Oh, you didn't have to do that.' Adrienne seemed uncomfortable.

'Yes, Dad, you didn't have to do that,' he said, shooting him a warning look.

His father simply brushed them both off. 'It's a thank-you more than anything, Your Highness.'

Franco pulled his lab coat open and let the cool breeze free on the skin around his neck. The heat was insufferable.

He shouldn't have mentioned anything at all to his father—why had he done that? He'd brought his family into her affairs by telling them about the bike accident. She would probably refuse the new one, he thought to himself. Too afraid her family would find out.

'A thank-you for what?' she asked. 'It was a huge mistake, what happened to the first one, and I really am so sorry—very embarrassed, actually,' she said, pulling her sunglasses down over her eyes.

'It wasn't exactly all your fault,' Franco muttered in her defence, trying not to smile. She was kind of cute when she apologised—especially in that lyrical Lisri accent of hers.

'It's not like you haven't done enough for us, Princess,' his father said now.

'I wouldn't refer to her as "Princess"—she hates it,' Franco warned him.

His father looked confused. 'But she *is* a princess.'

'I know,' he agreed, maybe a little too enthusiastically.

Perplexed, Marco dragged a hand through his hair, and Franco knew he'd be getting questions later.

'Anyway, Your Highness... Dr Balthus...'

'Just Adrienne, please.'

'Adrienne. Franco tells me it was you who arranged for a hefty annual donation to the Perretta Institute's research and development programme on behalf of your family and the Kingdom of Lisri. I want to invite you both to an event at the weekend. Some potential investors will be joining us on the yacht—some guys from the biotechnology lab in Florence, the new executive from the pharma leadership team. I thought we'd cruise around the Bay Islands...have dinner, drinks, maybe some music—you know how it goes. Franco can give a presentation on the results from the trials currently underway. And I'm inviting Allegra from the European Medicine Advisory Board. She's been a little busy lately, but—'

'Allegra should be doing more with her time than sailing about on yachts,' Franco cut in, looking towards Adrienne now. He knew his father was trying to be helpful—Franco had told him about their newest Ewing's sarcoma patient and the chemo drug still on trial. The advisory board was harder to reach than Mars, and he'd never even heard of this Allegra. 'We've hit yet another roadblock.'

'Well, let's unblock it,' his father said, as if pushing a drug trial through endless bureaucratic entanglements was as simple as flushing detergent down a drain.

'Maybe this Allegra is the key,' Adrienne mused.

Franco said nothing. He didn't want to come off as negative, but decisions like moving a trial forward from phase two to three took more than one person. It was a convoluted process, and this one had already been stalled for almost three years.

His father was still talking.

'I thought an illustrious attendee and backer such as yourself, Adrienne, might be...'

'What? Something to talk about?'

Franco got to his feet, lowering his voice as people turned to look at them on the forecourt. He was all too aware of how she loathed being paraded around like...what was it she'd said? A poodle in a dog show? He wouldn't put her on show here, too.

'Dad, Adrienne is here to work with our patients. I'm sure she doesn't want to stand up and—'

'What? Speak for myself?' Adrienne interrupted him.

He caught the warning glint in her eyes as she tossed her hair over her shoulders, and in a flash he was back among the cushions on her couch, her fingers tugging at his shirt, her lips possessing his mouth. He could still taste all her words, some sweeter than others: *'They want me to marry some baron now.'*

'I know what I said before, Franco, but this is important,' she continued.

'I need you to focus on your work,' he protested.

His father was looking between them, his grey eyebrows raised in interest. 'Do I sense something going on here?'

'No, you don't,' Franco said acerbically.

'The new bike is a very generous gift. Thank you, Mr Perretta,' Adrienne said quickly. 'You can have it sent to my address. Franco knows where I live.'

Franco's pulse throbbed in his neck. Adrienne stood tall, defiant, as his father poked his buzzing phone again, and he wondered if she'd fixed her ankle by willpower alone—she certainly hadn't let the injury slow her down...not that he'd let himself get close enough to her to check on it.

'I'd be happy to attend your dinner, Mr Perretta,' she added curtly. 'Now, if you'll both excuse me? I have another appointment.'

'Where?' Franco knew they both had a break before Candice Trentino was due for her latest immunotherapy treatment, but Adrienne was already swishing back through the doors.

'She's quite a woman,' his father said, watching her, bemused. 'Bet she keeps you on your toes.'

Franco dug his hands in his pockets and felt the usual blast of annoyance that stemmed from his unfortunate attraction to a woman who was already proving worse for his heart than anyone he'd ever met.

'She's working for me, Dad,' he said tautly.

His father chuckled and slapped him on the back. 'Working *on* you, more like.'

'What's that supposed to mean?' he growled.

'I may be getting older, son, but I'm not blind.'

CHAPTER THIRTEEN

WAITING FOR HER call from Bianca Caron to come in on her brand-new phone, Adrienne read her mother's latest letter, swivelling in her chair in the residents' room.

She'd already read it three times, in fear that she might have missed something about her housekeeper mentioning a man in her apartment—a man who'd scraped her off the side of the road after a motorcycle accident, no less. But it seemed Mirabel had kept her word, and the Queen was even being rather encouraging about her new project.

It sounds like this means a lot to you, Adrienne. And from the way you write about Dr Perretta it does seem as though you made the right move, going to Naples.

She should be relieved, but instead she just felt worse about Franco. Of course her mother didn't know how she wanted him to be more than her role model and mentor. If she told her mother about that kiss, she'd feel it was her duty to tell her husband—she told him *everything*. And what if Papa flew here himself, or sent someone from court to confront him, warn him off? Franco didn't deserve that humiliation.

Rather than insult him by keeping their time alone a secret, she'd done her best not to be alone with him at all. It went against every instinct, and every call from her fired-up libido.

His father knew, though.

Marco Perretta had definitely picked up on the tension between them, she thought, zoning out of reading the letter. The way Franco had acted outside just now, leaping to her defence... She hadn't needed him to stand up for her—she was doing fine on her own...most of the time. But she knew why he wanted her to refuse to help with progressing the trial: he felt the need to protect her from the spotlight after everything she'd told him.

He'd been acting as if they'd never kissed, and now this? Proof that he cared, whether he meant to show it or not. Her heart fluttered wildly again, just from thinking how she'd been putty in his big strong arms on her couch.

Her chiming phone pulled her from her reverie.

'Bianca, it's so good of you to agree to talk to me,' she said, walking to the door and closing it softly. She was alone. Just her and the palm trees whispering outside the window.

'It's not every day I get to speak to the Crown Princess of Lisri,' the twenty-one-year-old gushed.

Adrienne was quick to move on. 'I'm calling

as a doctor and donor to the Perretta Foundation,' she explained again, for the benefit of the cancer survivor's mother, who was also on the call.

She told them how she intended to share Bianca's story, along with the stories of others who'd seen encouraging results during phase two of the blocked trial, three years ago.

Her trusted cousin's media company was working on the website and the app, under the strictest of confidentiality agreements. The new organisation—Survive&Thrive—would be a safe space for patients and survivors to share their stories, which would be told from the heart, where Franco told *his* stories from. There would be links to helpful resources, real-life assistance on a live feed, updates on trials—the works.

It was coming together nicely. Soon she would have enough content to share—hopefully by the time they had to meet with that woman from the medical advisory board. She didn't know as much as Franco about the inner workings of it, but humans were humans, and hearts were hearts. Every story could move someone and make a difference.

'We need it moved on to phase three, so we can try to help more people,' she said now.

'Of course. I'm so excited to be a part of this.'

Maybe it wouldn't make a difference, she thought as Bianca waxed lyrical about the drug in the trial being the reason she was still alive and thriving. But maybe it would. Either way, it was better than sitting around on the phone, being put on hold, which was all Franco had been able to do so far.

Bianca seemed thrilled that people were about to read her story. 'I don't know why they blocked the same drug from being given to other people. It was only one person who experienced those side effects, and how those could be worse than cancer…that's just not possible!'

Candice had opted for immunotherapy treatment, and her new scans showed that her laryngeal cells seemed to be responding positively already, which only heightened Adrienne's buzz over her side project. She almost forgot the Franco-shaped elephant in the room, because she found herself so busy she barely had time to breathe.

Bianca had made firm friends with several of the other patients on the programme during her course of treatment and had promised to put Adrienne in touch with them. She knew she had a lot of work ahead of her, turning those accounts into moving, tangible evidence that the drug needed moving to phase three, but her mother's encouragement had lit a rocket under her, and she sped from the room after Candice had left, ready to get on the phone again.

Maybe she'd been softened by Adrienne's encouragement with her baking, but her mother hadn't mentioned the Baron's visit again. Perhaps she'd decided to forget she'd ever tried to set them up. Then again, maybe the Queen was biding her time before bringing it up again...with Papa's support, too.

Her mother's omission didn't sit right with Adrienne, now that she thought about it. She had mentioned Franco a lot in her last letter, and it didn't take a fool to fill in the gaps—as she was quite certain Marco Perretta had already.

No, Adrienne.

Her old anxieties were not permitted to follow her into this project. There was too much at stake.

Franco found her later, buried in a pile of notes and research papers in the residents' room. Her heart bolted as he closed the door behind him.

'What are you working on?'

'I'm writing discharge summaries. As well as about a thousand other things,' she replied truthfully as she felt the air grow thicker. He smelled like wood and citrus and sunshine. God, why did he have to be so gorgeous?

He perched on the edge of the desk opposite and eyed her thoughtfully. 'About my father's invitation,' he said. 'You don't have to come on the dinner excursion if you're too busy.'

She sat back in her seat. She should have expected this. He obviously didn't want her there, but she had to go. This wasn't about them. It was about patients like Rosita and getting the drug moved on in the trial, as well as the other contacts she'd meet.

'I'm coming.'

He nodded slowly, jaw clenched, then turned to the window.

'I thought perhaps this Allegra might help push our case with the board,' she added aloofly.

'I admire your enthusiasm, but let's not get excited. She's just one person, Adrienne.'

'We're all just one person, Franco,' she countered as he crossed to the window. 'Besides, I have an idea. I wasn't going to say anything yet, but—'

'I need you to focus on your work.'

Adrienne bristled. 'I am perfectly capable of multitasking.' She gestured to the pile of papers around her. 'And it sounds like you need me.'

Franco's mouth became a thin line.

'You don't have to protect me,' she said. 'I have Security for that.'

'I'm sure Ivan feels great, knowing he "protected you" from that motorcycle accident after you sent him off the other way.'

She stood tall, glaring at him as he rammed his hands through his hair.

'If you must know, I don't enjoy knowing the situation you're in, Adrienne. And this law that forbids you to marry anyone you damn well like is archaic.'

'There is no *law*, Franco,' she snapped in frustration. Then she lowered her voice as some people walked past outside the room. 'It's more of a tradition. Our family has always married other royals or high-ranking aristocrats.'

Franco looked confused.

'That's just the way it is,' she said. 'Other aristocrats understand what's expected of them as consort to a monarch, you see,' she explained. 'They understand the restrictions and the responsibilities…'

'Well, that's good, Adrienne. Because any *normal* person would just think that was crazy.'

Ouch.

With a jolt, she realised how much he must have been thinking about this since that night. She fought the urge to close the gap between them as he started pacing the floor and his shoes made heavy, frustrated smacks on the tiles. What was she supposed to do? Her life *was* crazy—and what did he want from her anyway?

'How can you live like that? Bending to everyone else's wishes?' he growled—to his shoes instead of her.

She swallowed tightly. 'I'm not married yet, am I?'

Franco stopped his pacing suddenly and strode purposefully towards her. She barely had time to catch her breath before his lips found hers, and in seconds they were kissing furiously again, sprawled on the desk, papers flying everywhere. She gasped, and then moaned into his mouth as he hoisted up her skirt, pressing a possessive hand to the flesh of her thigh and making her arch up into him.

The sound of footsteps behind the door caught her ears. He sprang away from her, pulling her upright, one fraction of a second before it swung open.

Irina came in and made for a pile of papers on another desk. 'Don't let me interrupt you, Doctors,' she said jubilantly, stopping to pause at the window for a second.

Adrienne waited. Her heart was a hammer under her coat. She must have seen something.

'What a beautiful day outside! Look at that sky! Oh, while I'm here, Adrienne, can you sign this? It's a leaving card for Matteo, for when he goes on paternity leave.'

Irina thrust a card showing a picture of a baby in a sling held in a stork's beak towards her and Adrienne took it with shaky hands, feeling her cheeks burn. So she hadn't seen them—thank goodness. That had been close. Too close. Franco had turned to the window, shoulders tense.

'I can only put my signature on official documents,' she said. 'Sorry.'

'Is that right?'

Adrienne caught Irina's look of disappointment, and yet again the fiery urge to dispel all the blue blood from her body consumed her. She had to remember who she was, but she was realising more and more by the second that who she *really* was had been pent up inside her for so long she barely recognised this whole new version of herself.

She snatched up a pen and wrote just her first name in block capitals.

'I hope he's looking forward to being a father,' she said of Matteo, their oncology social worker, handing the card back.

Franco had taken the opportunity to make his exit, leaving Adrienne hot and bothered even under the cool fan.

Irina tapped the door frame with the card on her way out. 'Is everything OK, Adrienne?' she asked. 'You look stressed. How is Candice?'

'Everything's fine,' she replied, resuming her cool, professional disposition. Although she was digging her nails so hard into her own palms they were leaving marks.

Irina closed the door after her and Adrienne could have kicked herself. She and Franco had almost been caught in an impassioned situation, here in their workplace, of all places. She really had to be more careful. There were eyes and ears everywhere…

But then, there always had been, and probably always would be. Wasn't that the problem? Franco wanted no part of that privacy invasion any more than he wanted to live by royal rules.

Her heart was on a dangerous path towards being a total wreck. She was still shaken by the kiss, and the smell of his cologne still lingered on her skin. That kiss had been as much her fault as his—they'd been winding each other up—but this had to end now. For both their sakes it must *not* happen again.

CHAPTER FOURTEEN

'WE HAVE TO be on the yacht with Dad in two days.'

Franco had stopped his bike under a tree to take Benni's call. He could hear Alina in the background. His brother had called to thank him for sending her the new spangly leotard and matching socks she'd asked him for, knowing full well her doting uncle would spoil her. And then Benni had swiftly moved the subject on to Adrienne.

'Is she definitely going to go with you? After you told me you were trying to stay away from her?'

'It will be good for her to be there,' Franco replied truthfully. 'But keeping it professional the whole time probably won't be easy. She's trying just as hard as me to pretend nothing has happened.'

'Are you sure?' Benni teased. 'Maybe one kiss from a frog scared her off if what she needs is a prince.'

'Two kisses, actually, and thanks a lot for calling me a frog.'

'Two? You went back for more? Are you crazy?'

'Maybe I am.' Franco watched a boat streak across the ocean under the blue sky, wishing the sweet scent of blossoming bougainvillea would calm his mind like it usually did.

'The woman is destined for a throne, Franco. What are you going to do? Move to Lisri with her and father her royal babies?'

Benni stifled a laugh at the thought, which hit a nerve.

'Of course not.'

He scowled at the ground, suddenly picturing another man by her side—someone she didn't even love. All for the sake of some outdated, ridiculous, hurtful tradition pushed upon her by the royal family.

Benni almost didn't even have to utter the words that came out next. 'Then walk away, bro. I'm warning you. This won't end well. You've already been through enough. Unless you can inject a few pints of blue blood into your veins, it's a lost cause.'

'Don't you think I know that? Besides, you should see what she has to go through, with her security and the paparazzi and...'

He trailed off, thinking how perhaps it wasn't all bad. She was strong and ambitious, and she had ideas on how to push the trial forward—not that she'd shared them yet. Which was probably his fault. He'd been all caught up trying to keep her out of the spotlight when actually she had every right to shine her light wherever she damn well wanted.

Benni was still talking. 'Don't walk, actually. Run. The last thing you want is the Lisri Prince Consort on your case, and I'll tell Dad to keep his nose out, too. He already seems to think you two have something going on.'

'Well, he's wrong.' Franco gritted his teeth as he looked at Vesuvius and the mountains looming before him like a judging jury. He was lying. To himself and to Benni. But the truth was tough to swallow. He was invested in Adrienne already—more than he wanted to be. And just this morning his father had insisted that they bring Adrienne's new bike aboard the yacht and go for a ride around Ischia.

'It can't all be about business, son. You have to do our country proud...make her want to sing its praises to her people. You can take her to the thermal baths.'

He could have put his foot down, told him not to meddle, but he hadn't. Maybe he *wanted* to take her there, just to see the look on her face. She'd love it. And damn if her smiles and excitement over all the new things he was showing her didn't give him new reasons to breathe.

For all the good it was doing him—or her.

'He just wants to see you happy again,' Benni told him. 'He doesn't care if she's the Crown Princess or if she stocks shelves all day in a supermarket. But I guess he doesn't know that her family only wants to marry her off into the aristocracy.' Benni paused. 'I don't want to encourage you when there's no hope whatsoever…but we all know plenty of people who consider you royalty anyway. And one of them is right here—isn't that right, Alina? Do you want to thank your uncle yourself for your new outfit before you cover it in grass stains?'

Thanks to his call with Benni and Alina, Franco was five minutes late for his shift, but Rosita and her family were also running late. Adrienne was exiting the residents' room when he passed, and she stopped in her tracks, as if she hadn't been expecting him to appear at all.

'Oh, you're here,' she said, flustered. 'I thought you were engaging with next-generation philanthropists at the university this morning.'

'I was,' he said, recalling the wide-eyed students he'd stood before in the lecture he'd been invited to lead. 'Then my brother called… What were you doing in there?'

He couldn't help his half-smile as she closed the door behind her as if she was shutting away a secret. She'd been hiding away in there a lot lately…on the phone, or huddled over her work. Probably keeping away from him, he thought wryly.

'Just another interview,' she explained, as if that explained anything.

'An interview? With who?'

'I'm working on something,' she replied evasively. 'It's not quite ready yet. I'll be more confident sharing when it is.'

'Try me,' he told her, intrigued.

Always a new mystery with you, Princess.

'How is it going, reaching the medical board about the trial?' she deflected, and he lowered his eyes, feeling the all too familiar bristling in his bones as he hit yet another brick wall.

'We should hear back in a few days.'

He walked with her towards the chemo lab. A kid walked past with his mother, stopping to stare at her from behind an IV pole, but Adrienne didn't even notice the attention.

'So, same as usual, then?'

'Pretty much. At least Rosita's tumour hasn't spread,' he said, examining the file she handed him as she opened the door for them. 'Regular chemo is better for Ewing's than it used to be. But as you know, if we can push phase three through and get her on board with the trial drug before the month is out, a mixture of the two might save her a few cycles.'

'Past results certainly seem to suggest that's the case,' she said thoughtfully.

Then she turned to him, fixing him with

gleaming blue eyes that threw his mind off course for just a second.

'Your father called me here this morning,' she said. 'He wants me to bring the new bike on board the yacht at the weekend. He seems to think you might be willing to show me the sights if we have a couple of hours spare.'

Franco didn't know whether to be amused or annoyed. 'I'm sure he does...' He exhaled, raking a hand through his hair. 'He must have called you right after he called me.'

'Do you think it's a good idea?' she asked him, and he paused, handing her back the file.

'That's up to you. Are you confident enough on a bike after what happened with the last one?'

His cheeks felt like they might crack with the force of his fake smile. He'd take her anywhere she wanted, but he probably shouldn't. If he did he would just speak his mind in the end, and look what that had led to last time—a make-out session on a desk...one that had almost got them both caught. It wasn't his place to question any unwritten rules of the Marx-Balthus family, or the Crown Princess's personal response to them.

'I wasn't talking about the bike,' she said, her long fingers playing with the pink stethoscope around her neck.

Her actions defied her bold statement—she was nervous, afraid she had pushed him away too hard. A certain helplessness tinged her stare, but he forced indifference.

'I know things have been…difficult recently. I didn't mean to make things awkward between us.'

'Let's just put what happened behind us, OK?' he said quickly, before she could break his resolve. 'You were right—it's for the best, all things considered. I shouldn't have kissed you again. Shall we go and see if Rosita's here?'

He continued walking, trying to ignore the slick of perspiration building on his brow at the lie. The 'best' thing to do was to keep things platonic…only no one had riled him up like this since Luci.

The truth was shouting at him more loudly, the more he tried not to hear it. As much as he'd loved her, Luci had never had him wanting her so desperately. Adrienne could break him harder than Luci ever had, with or without her family's help, and he simply didn't have the strength in him to lose someone else.

CHAPTER FIFTEEN

THE ISLANDS OF the Bay of Naples had been on her bucket list for a long time, but Adrienne was still not prepared for their beauty, even from a distance. A long weekend spent cruising around Procida, Ischia and Capri sounded ideal, but she wasn't just here for that, she reminded herself, stopping her Vespa by the dock and looking around her on the jetty for the others. The group of people she'd been expecting to meet prior to setting sail were nowhere in sight.

Her phone rang.

'Mother,' she answered, keeping her eyes on the crowds for stray cameras, as well as for Franco.

Ivan was lurking somewhere, watching for the same thing, but she was even more paranoid now. It had crossed her mind that maybe he'd seen Franco kiss her in the residents' room that time, even though she knew full well he'd been at the hospital gates outside. Her nerves were shot.

'How are you? I was expecting another letter. I know you hate the phone.'

'I just wanted to remind you that the Baron will be in Naples next week and he's looking forward to meeting you. You haven't mentioned when you'll be free.'

'I was hoping you'd forgotten about him,' she admitted, feeling hotter suddenly.

The Queen cleared her throat. 'Well, your papa has been asking me…'

'I'm sure he has, but he hasn't asked *me*.'

Adrienne frowned unseeingly into the crowds. She should have known her mother's silence on the topic was too good to be true. Now Papa was making her chase her down on the issue. He probably didn't want it to seem like *he* was pushing her. Typical. Their relationship had been tenuous at best, since his comment about a lying, cheating user like Xavier still being an excellent match because of his royal blood.

The Queen was quiet for a moment. Then she took Adrienne by surprise. 'How are things with that fine doctor? Dr Perretta? Have you told him your big idea yet? I happen to think it's marvellous, what you're doing. You could help a lot of people through this—'

'I'm up here!'

Franco's voice behind her took the air from her lungs.

'Mother, I'm sorry, I have to go.'

She hung up, heart fluttering, and turned to see him standing on the front lower deck of the yacht behind her, holding up a hand. His white shirt was open at the front, and he looked every inch the yachtsman who'd sailed to Capri with a pod of dolphins in his wake.

This was the yacht they'd be spending the weekend on? It had at least three decks, and a swimming pool she could see from the pier.

The breeze caught his hair and she forgot the conversation with her mother, noting with dismay how he looked sexier than ever against the turquoise water and the stark white exterior of the glamorous vessel.

'Princess Adrienne of Lisri? Is that you?'

Oh, no. Someone was calling to her from another boat, and within seconds a crowd of people had recognised her in spite of her headscarf. She looked up to the yacht again for Franco, but he was gone.

At first she panicked, as was her standard reaction, but then she reminded herself sternly that she was no longer accepting a life where her true self was squashed into the shadows.

'Of course you can have a photo,' she said to the lady who had stopped by her bike, wielding a camera.

Surprisingly, it felt nice to give a few people something they wanted instead of updates on their tumours. And even the Queen was excited by her involvement at the institute. Her mother had certainly sounded a little less enthusiastic than usual about meddling in her love life.

By the time Franco reached her she was busy

signing tourist leaflets, with Ivan looming over the proceedings, and explaining to the people who had gathered how she was there as a doctor, working on cancer research amongst other things.

'Are you OK?' Franco seemed concerned as he moved to make a shield of himself between her and a young boy who'd run up to her on behalf of his bashful older brother. 'Allegra has had something important come up, so Dad wants us to meet later instead,' he said.

'That's no problem. And, yes, I'm absolutely fine, thank you,' she replied, moving him aside to sign the kid's map.

'You want me to leave you here?' he asked, one eyebrow cocked in amusement.

She considered saying yes, but as more people gathered she thought better of it—even with Ivan there. A little attention wasn't a bad thing, but she didn't want to look as if she was encouraging some kind of celebrity status.

The adrenaline rush hadn't subsided by the time Franco and a deckhand named Diego had steered her bike onboard to a special garage on the bottom level of the yacht. Franco's was parked there already.

'You didn't seem to mind the attention that time,' Franco observed, checking her brakes and tyres.

'I guess it's all part of the job. Or should that be jobs?' she said, removing her headscarf and shaking her hair loose. 'I have many roles—as do you, Franco, am I right? How's your niece doing?'

He seized the opportunity to talk about Alina and sent Diego off, saying he would handle her luggage. She studied Franco's biceps, filling out his shirtsleeves, thinking he was just as passionate about his role as Alina's uncle as anything else he threw his heart and soul into. For the first time she imagined he'd be a great dad someday, then admonished herself quickly for daring to fantasise that she herself might bear his children.

This is where it stops, she warned herself yet again. There was no point indulging in any fantasies about Franco. Things were too complicated as it was. In fact, she should distance herself as much as would be possible on a boat.

'I should get back to work,' she told him. 'I assume this vessel has a study?'

'Is this your secret project that you still haven't shared?' he replied, brushing off her mention of working in the study.

She nodded as her pulse spiked. 'It's almost ready.'

'I'm intrigued,' Franco muttered, shutting her bike seat down over the spare helmet and medical kit inside.

She didn't know quite how to take that, but then again she was distracted by his biceps as he screwed the oil cap tighter and then gestured her to follow him back outside.

* * *

'Wow!' she heard herself say suddenly.

Franco had led her up a flight of polished wooden stairs to the second outer deck, where three more staff members were waiting behind a swim-up bar adorned with orchids and candles in jars. The rippling swimming pool was bluer than the sea beyond, and the cream-coloured oval lounge chairs, each with a single plush orange cushion on, quickly pushed all thoughts of work from her head.

'This is magical,' she gushed, allowing the romance of the setting to sink in in spite of herself.

Franco led her to the bar as a staff member dressed all in white slid two pre-made margaritas towards them. Marilyn Monroe smiled seductively from a pop art print behind him.

Something in the back of her head told her to insist she get back to work, but she couldn't quite make the words leave her mouth.

'Welcome to the *Lady Fatima*.' He clinked his glass against hers. 'It's the second yacht I co-bought with Dad and Benni. It's for entertainment, mostly.'

'Where's the first?' she asked, noting the extravagant indoor entertainment space beyond the giant double doors behind the bar. There was a piano, a dance floor, another bar, a table for at least fifteen people, and opulent chandeliers dangling over centrepiece arrangements of fruit and more flowers.

'The first was auctioned off. We put the proceeds into the Perretta Institute to fund the trial. Phase one and phase two.'

He slid out two white stools and she sat, noting the cool white leather and embroidered stitches—multi-millionaire touches she actually hadn't expected, now that she thought about it. Franco usually wore his wealth like an old sweater... like something that was comfy but nothing to show off about.

His knee brushed hers below the bar and she felt the deep rumble of the yacht's engines before she noticed they were leaving the harbour already.

'Would you sell this too? If it meant phase three could go ahead?' she asked him, already knowing the answer.

'You know I would. But like I said, it's not about money. It's about breaking down bureaucratic barriers, and unfortunately we're dealing with hundred-foot steel walls here. I'm starting to think we won't get Rosita or any other patient on that trial anytime soon.'

'Don't think that,' she said, watching him trail a thumb idly around the salted rim of his glass.

His defeated tone made her want to tell him about her project now. But she'd share it soon enough. He put the glass to his lips and took a sip of his drink, and she saw new sunlit hues in the deep green depths of his eyes, and faint lines born of all those emotions he either expressed with passion or bottled up till they exploded. She'd infuriated him recently—she knew it, and she felt terrible.

Did anyone here see it? she wondered. This fizzing, bubbling champagne concoction of beautiful chemistry? Had her mother seen it in her letters? Was that why she'd changed the subject from the Baron to Franco in their phone call earlier?

Her heart sped up just at thinking of her mother telling her father. If she could, she would tell her mother everything. She'd shout her feelings from the royal rooftops. But she couldn't risk anyone coming down hard on Franco. He hadn't done anything wrong—and besides, it would jeopardise her project and the trial even more.

Just her presence in his life could be his downfall, she thought, her eyes shifting to Ivan, who'd taken up residence on a lounger at the other end of the deck.

Two staff members were standing over by the lifeboats, staring at her, speaking in lowered voices. She sipped her drink again, looking straight at them, till they scurried off, embarrassed.

'So, Franco...' she straightened up '...if you have some time later to discuss...?'

'We have all day now,' he said, a little wearily. 'But maybe we shouldn't think about work for a little while. Personally, I need a break.'

Crossing her legs in her tailor-made scarlet culottes, she found their knees touching again as they sipped their drinks in silence. Neither of them moved. Hot electricity zinged between them as she let her eyes run up the faint smattering of dark hair revealed by his unbuttoned shirt and he tried to pretend he didn't see her looking.

'If you insist,' she replied coolly, in spite of herself.

She would have thought he'd need a break from her too, but although he seemed unhappy about her being here, he hadn't put his authoritative foot down as he might have done. It struck her suddenly that Marco Perretta might have set this up on purpose. Maybe their fathers weren't so very different after all.

The thought of presenting Survive&Thrive to Franco filled her with hot anticipation as they made small talk about the yacht and the staff. She was proud of her work, and of the kids, teens and adults who'd so bravely told their stories. Of the medical professionals who'd consented to give their time and share their experience.

She would have told him sooner, but she'd only just completed the final interview that morning. The web designer was working on the finishing touches, and she was expecting to give the green light on it at any moment. It had to look perfect if it was going to be a success.

Franco was still watching her over his glass. He wasn't thinking about work. He was thinking about her. She could feel it. Drinking cocktails probably wasn't wise…

She put her drink down, mostly un-drunk, and as if reading her mind Franco did the same, and then told her he would show her around the yacht.

Adrienne followed him into a stateroom, feeling the tension snake around them as Franco placed her weekend bag on the king-size bed. It was adorned with golden and white cushions to match the window drapes. Brass and marble features stretched from the bedframe to the taps and tiles as he showed her the en suite bathroom with an impressive power shower.

'It's a little ostentatious, I know…sorry', he apologised, pointing out a display board of buttons next to the control that operated at least four different shower heads.

'It's more like a car wash,' she agreed, fighting a smile, and then went back to examining the embroidered towels as he pulled out his phone and frowned into it.

'I've been on fancier boats—if you can believe that,' she commented, wondering who it was that could be winding him up now. 'That must make me sound like a yacht snob, but…'

'I can only imagine what kind of royal vessels

the monarchy keeps at its disposal in Lisri,' he said, sliding his phone back into the pocket of his low-slung denim shorts.

Suddenly they were face to face in the silence of the bathroom, and the walls, solid white marble, felt as if they were closing in.

'Did you have many men take you on dates out on the open water?' he questioned. 'Maybe a baron on a sailing boat? A duke on a speedboat?'

'No...' she replied after a pause.

She knew she had wounded his pride, explaining how her family had a strong preference for royalty and noblemen, but his words stung. It wasn't as if she *wanted* the loveless marriage she was probably destined for in the end.

She stuck out her chin, determined not to show how he was getting to her. 'I think I told you before we met,' she said, 'how I learned to sail when I was twelve.'

'No, you didn't,' he said, and she remembered that she actually hadn't. She'd just read about how *he* liked to sail and imagined the rest.

'I don't need a man to take me,' she told him stiffly.

Franco's mouth twitched. He corrected the alignment of a slightly wonky picture of a scene from a James Bond movie on the wall by the round porthole window. Outside the ocean sparkled and the sun beat down hard with the call of freedom.

'Good. We don't have sails, but I'll put you in charge of the lifeboats if we need them.'

'Gladly.'

She made for the door. Suddenly she needed the breeze on her face. Air. Space.

Hot on her heels he caught her elbow, just as she made to leave the suite.

'That was out of line. I'm sorry,' he said on an exhalation, turning her to face him. 'I'm just… That was a message from another contact at the advisory board. He promised to try and move things on, but he's having no luck. More delays.'

She bit her tongue.

Diego appeared at the end of the row of state-rooms, holding a pile of towels, and pretended not to notice them.

She lowered her voice. 'It's not just the trial that's getting to you.'

He looked surprised for a second—maybe even more surprised than *she* was to have said it out loud. Then his face darkened again. 'I don't know what you want from me, Adrienne.'

'Nothing,' she said—too quickly.

'Sometimes I think you want nothing. But sometimes I think you want a whole lot more.'

'And what about you?' she countered.

Right away she regretted it. He fixed her a with a piercing look that sawed right through her. She could tell he wanted her, but he was just as wary of getting hurt as she was because of Lucinda.

He'd been hurt as much as Adrienne—for different reasons, absolutely, but pain was pain.

He was probably also wondering what the hell his life might entail if he entangled himself in her world even more. A private man and a dedicated doctor like Franco Perretta wouldn't be able to suddenly leave it all behind and become a ribbon-cutting prince, especially after glimpsing how complicated everything was in the goldfish bowl she called her life.

'Maybe it wasn't such a good idea for me to come here,' she said quickly. 'That's what you're thinking, right?'

'It's not what I'm thinking.'

Franco stepped so close she could feel his breath on her skin. In a flash she was back to that night on the couch in her apartment, and then their passionate kiss in the residents room. It was as if magnets had taken over again, and pushed all sense and reasoning aside.

He cupped her chin, traced a tender thumb over her lower lip that caused a sharp moan to escape her mouth. Time seemed to freeze. Her resolve was wilting in the heat of his stare. But before she could surrender completely and press her mouth to his delicious lips he broke contact...killed the moment.

He swiped a key card in the door opposite hers and she ran her fingers over her lips, catching her breath, absorbing his touch. Torture. He'd been about to kiss her again, but of course had thought better of it. She watched him throw his shoes inside the stateroom and slip on a different pair before closing the door again, heavily.

Wait.

He was sleeping in the room right opposite hers?

Her heart was already in her throat. Fresh need and lust tingled through her.

She would lie there alone in that bed tonight, seeing herself wrapped around him, both of them tangled in clean silky sheets, with the sound of the ocean lapping the boat through the open windows, the cool night-time breeze caressing every inch of their naked skin.

She would lie there imagining herself locked against that solid muscled chest, knowing she'd have to resist all her urges to go to him for real, denying herself his touch once again…if he would even go near her now she'd built her defences up so high.

For his own good.

This was hell.

He led her around the yacht, making small talk in front of the staff they came across.

He pointed out the games room, stocked with a pool table and more books than she'd ever owned or read. Then took her through the cinema room and another lounge with a marble chess board, a study overlooking a tempting outdoor hot tub, and on through the engine room, where he explained engine power and the twelve-point-five-knot cruising speed.

All the while she couldn't stop imagining him sleeping in that room opposite hers tonight. Did he sleep naked? Did he make gentle noises while he dreamed? Did he ever dream of her, or did he wish they'd never met?

A wave of fatigue washed over her, just from thinking of the long evening and the weekend ahead.

CHAPTER SIXTEEN

'Twenty-five centuries to its name,' Franco said over his shoulder as Adrienne trailed him slowly on the Vespa along the path leading up to the mighty Aragonese Castle. 'If walls could only talk.'

'I'm sure they'd have a few secrets to tell,' she said, fixing her eyes on the islet ahead, which had formed some three hundred thousand years ago after an eruption, to create a giant hill that protruded from the ocean.

Adrienne had seemed quietly enamoured of what he'd shown her of Ischia so far, even though things between them were awkward, to say the least. He'd taken her through Ischia Ponte, the oldest village on the islands, where they'd explored quiet back lanes and classic Mediterranean architecture. Then they'd sipped cold drinks on a jasmine-scented terrace, and he'd attempted to lighten the mood with more myths and legends about this very castle.

But the almost-kiss was still on his mind. He'd stopped himself, though he had the impression she'd been about to initiate more this time.

'They say that if you kiss someone here you'll be with them for ever,' he'd said at one point. Then he'd wanted to kick himself. The Princess was the wrong audience for such a romantic fact—especially now.

She'd let him fill the silence with more stories, but she hadn't asked him any questions like she usually did. She'd checked her watch every now and then, as if she was counting down the minutes till she could escape.

They'd only be stuck on the yacht, though, if they turned around. That would be even more awkward, with the staff loitering around, listening out for gossip on the Crown Princess, and Ivan, who was probably behind them now, trying to appear inconspicuous.

He would keep quiet from now on. He shouldn't have made that dig earlier about her going sailing with some baron or duke or whatever, but the thought of her enduring dates for the sake of some ancient family tradition still had him just as riled up as the stagnation they were experiencing around the trial. And all the tension between them whenever they were alone wasn't helping. Especially in that bedroom…

God, if only she knew how much he'd longed to press her down into that mattress and show her the kind of night he'd been fantasising about since he'd met her. Self-solace just wasn't enough any more.

Not helping, Franco, he chided himself. It was hot enough out here already.

They drove on towards the castle, past idling tourists in sunhats and couples posing for photos with the ocean-blue backdrop. Adrienne overtook him and he watched the back of her, memorising her shape, the golden strands of her hair, reminding himself he'd done the right thing at least by not kissing her earlier.

But just the thought of her settling for some bog-standard, insipid baron just to appease her family made him feel sick to the core. Life was short and precious. It should be a rollercoaster ride, not a slow, drawn-out process of suffocation.

They toured the castle rooms and Adrienne took photos with her phone of the views from various precipices. Each window offered amazing panoramas of Procida and Ischia Ponte, but a call from the institute took him outside alone for a moment. He'd asked for updates, and was grateful now for something to take his mind off Adrienne.

It was as if they were stuck between this huge castle rock and a hard place, he thought to himself as Irina chattered on in his ear. There was nothing much new for her to report, and he was instructed to enjoy his weekend off.

Frowning to himself, he turned on the path to find Adrienne watching the swimmers down below, her red culottes billowing in the breeze, her hair blowing in gentle wisps about her neck.

Picture-perfect. Without thinking, he snapped a photo of her against the sky.

'What are you doing?'

'I'll delete it,' he said quickly, embarrassed that he'd done it without asking, like some awestruck fan out on the street. 'You just looked…hot.'

She sighed. 'I am hot…and maybe a little bothered too,' she said, missing the double entendre and wafting her cotton shirt around her breasts, using one hand as a fan. 'I don't like this tension between us. We should be doing something else. Maybe we should just go back to the yacht and I'll show you what I've been working on.'

'It sounds important.'

'It could be,' she said, chewing her lip.

A rush of guilt swept through him over being so caught up in the trial—and in trying to stay away from her—that he hadn't even given her a chance to explain herself regarding whatever it was she'd been pouring all her hours into lately.

The sky was darkening with the threat of rain. He knew it would shift the humidity. Maybe they should get back to the yacht, where they could stay dry and she could walk him through her project. But then again, what was one more hour? He should at least show her the best part of the island…

Adrienne removed her helmet and took in the sparkling rocks and pebbles in the pools of hot water just back from the beach, with their vents of steam billowing up from the sea floor.

'Some people say they're healing waters,' he explained as they parked their bikes on a grassy patch overlooking the bay below. 'All you need is a few minutes in them.'

'That's a prescription I wouldn't mind receiving.'

'Well, be my guest,' he said, pointing to a small changing facility, where she could get into her bathing suit. 'I'll be in the water, over there.'

Franco took off his shirt and stuffed it underneath his bike seat, grateful for the chance to get into the water—maybe it would help his brain this time, he thought, more than his bones.

When he turned, Adrienne was still watching him from behind her sunglasses. He caught her eyes roving his body in what looked a lot like silent appreciation for just a split second before she hurried off in the direction of the changing room. He bit back a pleased smile and headed across the pebbles for the pool with the least people in it.

Pools like this were scattered among the coastal rocks all over the island and bubbled at temperatures between thirty and thirty-seven degrees all year round. He'd brought Luci here once, just to try it, to see if it would ease some of her pain. It had worked its magic for an hour or two. Not long enough, unfortunately, he remembered.

Franco was just relaxing into a warm, rocky

nook, with the water up to his shoulders, when Adrienne reappeared. All thoughts of Luci slipped straight from his brain.

'This was such a great idea,' she told him as his eyes travelled up her long, lean legs from bare feet to glistening thighs. She put her bag down on the rocks. He knew damn well she was giving him time to take in her body, slender and yoga-toned in a blue and green bathing suit. It was the cruellest act of torture.

'There are better places like this along the coast,' he told her, trying to sound indifferent to the fact that something most unfortunate was happening to his lower body beneath the steam. 'I know pools that only boats can reach.'

'Mmm…' she mumbled, and slid like a slick dolphin into the water.

A rumble of thunder warned them that the change in weather was getting closer, but Adrienne dipped her head underwater, the very picture of the calm before the storm. Her hair fanned around her head before she came up with her eyes closed. Droplets clung to her eyelashes as she blinked.

'This is just what I needed,' she breathed, just as he was wondering how on earth he'd ever be able to leave the pool with her looking like that next to him.

For a few long minutes they sat in silence. The rain was now falling and making tiny ripples in the water. They were both stealing glances at each other through the steam.

'I don't like all this tension around us either,' he said after a moment. 'But I hope you're at least glad you got to see this place.'

'Of course.'

Then she frowned, casting steely eyes at a few people who'd stepped closer in their direction. It was as if he saw the cogs turning. She'd insisted Ivan stay back by the road, to keep a watch for any big groups arriving.

'Don't worry,' he said. 'No one will recognise you like that. Besides, you're out with a regular guy like me, so who'd pay us any attention?'

Another dig. He couldn't help it. Just seeing her like this was infuriating, knowing he could look but not touch.

'There's nothing regular about you, Franco, and you know it,' she said tartly. Then she stuck up her toes in the water between them, wriggling them with satisfaction. 'For what it's worth, I feel honoured every time you take me anywhere.'

'But would you tell anyone back home that?' he asked, then immediately wished he hadn't. Why was he digging this hole for himself even deeper?

She sighed, drawing his eyes to her cleavage as she swept a wet tendril of hair back behind her ear. 'I talk to my mother, actually,' she said. 'About some things. I've talked to her more than I ever have before, lately. Sometimes I feel like she regrets the life she's been forced into. I think she's happy for me that I'm here…away from all that, seeing all these things.'

Franco felt his eyes narrow. '*Forced* into?'

Adrienne shook her head, as if she already regretted her words. 'That came out wrong. I mean, she loves Papa dearly—always has. But she inherited the throne so young, you know? She's never been expected to work, or to cook—even though she's an excellent baker—or to travel alone, or even to think too much for herself…'

'Whereas you will become a doctor,' he finished. 'Will you be able to practise when you take the crown?'

He'd never asked her before. He'd assumed she'd be too involved in other things when her time on the throne came, but she was frowning at him now.

'I'll do whatever I like with my days—including practising medicine—as long as it's for the good of my country. I have a list of things I'm going to do for Lisri and, trust me, it grows longer every day.' She looked at him sideways. 'But the Queen isn't going anywhere for a long time yet. Decades. So I have plenty of time. And she's taking notes from me, even if she doesn't say it. Papa too. They like to think they're not old-fashioned but…you know.'

He bit back a smile, struck by this different side to her. She was a superstar, challenging the paradigm of what a crown princess should be and do. This was a woman on track for a bright future, and she'd have it with or without a man.

'You really can do anything you want to do with power like that,' he heard himself say.

She smiled, lifting the tension. 'It's not all bad, is it?'

'You're going to change so many lives.'

'Well, it's not like *you* don't do that already, Franco.'

'Oh, my God, Emma? Where's Emma? Have you seen her?'

The panicked cry made them both turn to the next pool in shock.

A young woman was scrambling from the water ten feet or so away. Almost instantly she was lost in the steam. 'My daughter—she was just here, have you seen her?'

Frantically, the woman in a red two-piece bathing suit searched around her, asking everyone in sight, almost sliding on the increasingly wet rocks around the pools in her hurry.

'Be careful!' Franco yelled at her, heaving himself from the pool with his forearms in one swift movement. He turned to help Adrienne, but she was already hot on his heels.

'She was just here—right here. Emma!'

'How old is she? What does she look like?'

Adrienne had crossed the slippery rocks with speed to reach the woman alongside him. A crash of thunder slashed through the scene and impulsively he put an arm out to steady Adrienne. This place could be dangerous. Unsupervised children could wander off and get into trouble pretty fast—especially in weather like this, which was getting worse.

The woman was barely able to speak. Her dark panic-stricken eyes were darting this way and that, trying to locate her daughter. 'She's three,' she managed.

'What is she wearing?'

'Yellow bathing suit. She's hard to miss but I don't see her... Oh, my God, where is she...? She can't swim.'

Franco cast his eyes out to the ocean, scanning the horizon. The rain was coming down more heavily now, beating the ground in angry smacks. The steam made visibility almost zero, and the wind was throwing salty spray into their eyes, not helping matters at all.

'When did you last see her?' he asked.

'I was getting her drink from my bag. When I turned around she was gone. Less than two minutes ago, I swear.'

'Over here!' Another voice came from the shoreline. 'I think I saw something. I think she's in the water!'

Beside him, Adrienne and the girl's mother both almost slipped in their haste to get to the oceanfront.

'Be careful!' Franco called out as he followed them, watching in case they fell.

The last thing they needed was broken and twisted limbs, on top of a missing child, but Adrienne was already scrambling towards the sand.

'She's in the water!' she gasped in horror, just as he spotted a flash of yellow disappear beneath a wave.

Time froze.

'Emma!'

The distraught woman did her best to run into the raging water, but she shrieked as she was pushed back—half by a threatening wave, and half by Adrienne.

'It's too dangerous!' he heard her cry. 'Franco, where's the lifeguard?'

There was no lifeguard. He knew that. People were supposed to watch themselves around here…and their kids.

Several families were hovering around on the periphery of the sea now, squinting through the rain, observing the scene in shock. In the distance he could see Ivan, already on his phone to someone.

Franco didn't wait for the young girl's bathing suit to reappear in the water. Without thinking, he leapt into the ferocious waves and started swimming.

CHAPTER SEVENTEEN

BEFORE A CRY could escape her lungs, Franco was being smothered by a wave three times his height. Adrienne watched in horror, forcing her mouth not to emit the shrieks and urgent cries she felt building up inside her.

He was a strong swimmer—he had told her that once, when he'd talked about jumping off the yacht to swim with those dolphins. But now the sky was a deep, unforgiving grey and the lashing rain formed a cloak, concealing him from her view.

'Emma…oh, Emma.'

Beside her, the little girl's mother had her hands over her mouth and was sinking slowly to the wet sand on her knees, letting the violent surf wash up and over her lap.

'My baby…my baby…' she repeated, rocking herself slowly even as Adrienne tried to urge her backwards, before she got swept away too.

She yelled out for someone to call emergency services, but they already had—probably Ivan, she thought, catching him holding a hand up to her. She could hear a siren somewhere in the distance and she motioned to him to stay back, not to draw attention to her in the middle of all this.

She prayed it wasn't too late for the little girl. The toddler would have been swept so far out by now that even if Franco could get to her, who knew how much water she might have sucked into her tiny lungs in a frantic effort to get back to her mother?

'Where are they? I don't see anything!'

'It's OK…he *will* find her,' Adrienne promised, praying that by saying it, by promising it, she'd persuade whatever God might be up there to take it as a firm instruction to, please, let him find the child.

It felt as if an eternity passed as she stood there, scanning every frothy white crest of a wave for a hand, or a foot, or a flash of yellow like before. A bigger crowd had gathered along the shoreline, and several other guys had attempted to go in, but the waves were too big, propelling them backwards as fast as they could swim out.

'I have to go in!'

The mother scrambled to her feet and almost fell straight on to her face as another wave rushed at her, like an angry wolf guarding its cubs from a stranger.

Adrienne held her back with brute strength. 'Don't. It's not safe. I've told you he'll find her.'

'Then where are they?'

Adrienne felt sick, still holding her back. It

took every ounce of her strength not to follow him in herself. But she was not a strong swimmer; she had always been more interested in sailing a boat than jumping off its bow.

She prayed with more fervour, ordering, begging, silently scanning the horizon for signs of Emma and Franco. Relentless waves crashed and rushed at them, hitting the shore but bearing no sweet gifts of life, no Franco, no Emma.

Please, please, let them both be safe. I don't want to lose him. Please.

Suddenly…

'Franco!'

He appeared like some kind of merman, head first, then full torso. He was ten feet away, bobbing in the water and catching his breath. The girl's yellow swimsuit was a beacon in his arms, and the woman's harrowing sobs of fear and relief combined made the crowd gasp, then cheer, as Franco started swimming towards them.

He was swallowed again in a second by another wave, and several other guys waded in to help him. Adrienne got waist-deep herself before she was lifted by a current she hadn't even known was there. Suddenly there were no coordinated movements—just her hands and feet clawing through seawater to regain some kind of stability.

Oh, God, what had she done?

She tried to yell out, but she was dragged under and her mouth filled with water.

Someone was grabbing her. A big, burly, broad-shouldered guy, with a face half obscured by a greying beard, scooped her up in his arms as he would cradle a newborn baby.

'P-Princess?' he stuttered in alarm—just before he ducked them both below an approaching wave to avoid being smashed by it.

Franco was almost at the shore when she came up, gasping for air. 'Put me down,' she spluttered at her saviour, and he did so immediately, shocked. 'Thank you,' she remembered to say, as her feet found sandy ground.

Sweeping wet hair from her eyes, she waded towards Emma's mother, scanning the beach for Franco. He was fast approaching, carrying the child in his arms, abdominals straining.

'She's not breathing,' he told her, as quietly as he could in the chaos. 'Stand back!' he yelled at the others. 'We need some room here. We're doctors.'

'Someone get that backpack!' she called out, pointing to the bag she'd left by the pool.

She was still panting heavily, and doubly drenched by the now torrential rain. The sirens wailed closer now and she caught her breath, coughing the whole time. Impatience made her brush away someone's hand when they came to help her. All she could think about was Emma.

The paramedics would have to scramble down the slope, across the wet rocks. It would all take time they didn't have to lose. The young girl's pretty face was too still. Her eyes were closed and unblinking.

Shaken, Adrienne helped Franco lay her down on the wet sand as someone else put down a towel for her.

The burly guy who'd recognised her held Emma's mother back, watching from the sidelines in a way that would have made Adrienne uncomfortable if Ivan hadn't been close, and if she hadn't been completely absorbed by the situation. He seemed to be the only one who'd recognised her, but she wasn't exactly the focal point here.

The poor woman was sobbing wretchedly. 'My baby, my baby...please, help her.'

'I'm going for CPR,' Franco said, and cleared her airway as best he could.

She watched in a daze as wet jet-black hair tumbled over his forehead. Her bag was delivered from by the pool, tossed to her across the rocks. She scrambled for it as his hands started pumping at the girl's tiny flat chest, praying for a spark, just a tiny movement that would tell them it wasn't too late.

'Emma, my Emma...please, you have to help her.'

Painful pressure built in her throat as she watched the scene unfold like a dream, fighting back tears. Franco's hands looked so big across the child's small, fragile frame.

One… Two… Three… Nothing was helping.

She watched Franco start CPR again. *Please. Please.*

It felt like an eternity in the lashing rain before Emma coughed and contracted beneath him. Then she bolted upright, tears pooling in her fluttering eyes, coughing and spluttering up salt water.

Franco fell on to his backside on the rocks in relief as the crowd cheered in unison. Her mother rushed over and swept the child into her arms, just as the paramedics arrived on the slippery scene with a spine board.

For the first time, Adrienne caught sight of the line of people who'd gathered at the curve of the bay, back where they'd parked the bikes.

Where had all those people *come* from?

The next fifteen minutes were a blur of statements and forms and tears and thank-yous. By the time the ambulance had driven off with Emma, thankfully the rain was subsiding—along with the crowds—but Adrienne had a headache from coughing too much and squinting through the rain.

When she turned, exhausted and emotional, the bearded ox-like man who'd pulled her out from under wave was staring at her, pointing a camera. Her heart leapt into her throat.

'Let's get out of here.'

Franco was walking up behind her. He must have escaped the gushing praise of a young girl in a blue bikini who'd managed to win his attention after the paramedics had left. Tracking the camera still aimed at her, she almost slid on the rocks again.

'Careful!'

Franco's strong hands gripped her shoulders, steadying her. His face reflected none of the emotion making jelly of her limbs.

He slung the backpack onto his broad shoulders, then grazed her cheek with one palm, turning her face, as if to inspect it for damages. The gentle touch sent a tingling rush through her stomach. Impulsively, distracted, she pressed her own hand over his, trying to forget the way she'd seen her whole life flash before her eyes when she'd lost him, and then herself, beneath the waves.

'Are you all right to drive?'

Remembering the man with the camera, she pulled away too quickly. She watched Franco's damp, bronzed face darken like the passing storm when he saw the guy in red shorts. His lens was now directed at both of them, and she was still exposed in her swimsuit.

'Hey! You! Put that away!' Enraged, Franco

started off towards him, but the guy was already scrambling across the rocks to escape. 'You'd better delete those pictures!' he called after him, but before they could reach him, he'd set off on his own motorcycle and was speeding back towards the castle.

CHAPTER EIGHTEEN

IN THE CORRIDOR on the second deck, a couple of hours later, Franco caught Adrienne leaning against the wall outside her stateroom, eyes closed, hugging herself. He'd come to find her after she'd taken two sips of her drink, then disappeared from the group around the bar, shooting him a look that implied she wanted him to follow her.

'I need to talk to you,' she said when she saw him. 'I didn't want to say anything in front of your father, or any of the others.'

'We can talk,' he said, turned on by just the scent of her shower gel, still lingering on her skin. Its fresh, nuanced blend of lilies and roses with a subtle, underlying note of white musk filled his nostrils. It somehow matched the white cotton dress she'd slipped on for the evening, and for a second it pressed a delete key on the events at the pools.

They were still all talking about it upstairs. No news reporters had been at the scene, but a couple of eyewitnesses had spoken about what they'd seen. So far none of them had recognised Adrienne, except the guy who'd taken her photo, and

Franco hoped for her sake that he'd keep the photos for his private collection and leave the press out of it. The last thing she needed was pictures of herself in a swimsuit all over the Internet, and *he* didn't need to be seen standing like that next to her, either.

'That was pretty crazy, what just happened,' he said. She was looking at a framed print on the wall. 'We don't have to go back up there, you know. They're not expecting anything from you.' He studied the print alongside her, surprised to see a look of slight offence in her eyes when she glanced at him. 'I meant after what happened,' he added. 'They know you're tired, Adrienne, why don't you just rest?'

She ignored him and pulled her key card out from the tiny leather bag across her shoulder. 'I'll rest later.'

He watched her gather her laptop and some papers from the desk, while the width and squishy comfort of the inviting bed tortured him from where he remained in the doorway.

'Your father thinks the moon and stars of you,' she said, jamming her laptop into a leather bag with some cables. 'And everyone out there thinks you're a hero for going into those waves when the sea was…like that.'

He caught her eyes in the mirror on the wall, watching him…watching her. He felt a 'but' coming on.

'But you did a reckless thing. You had no life-buoy, no nothing, Franco.'

'What did you want me to do? Let her drown?' He half laughed.

She raked a hand through her hair in frustration. 'Of course not! You can't know what went through my head this afternoon.'

'Maybe you're wrong about that,' he said as his jaw began to tick. 'You went off to find a kitten and left me thinking you'd plunged straight off a cliff.'

'It's not a competition,' she retorted, moving as if to press her hands to his chest and seeming to think better of it.

Just the almost-touch sent a lightning bolt of desire right through him, and maybe her too, because to his complete surprise she reached up with stormy eyes and pressed her mouth to his, falling hard against him as he pulled her in. He kissed her back hungrily, till she was breathing hot and hard against his parted lips, arching into him with her back to the wall.

'Adrienne…'

'Don't,' she said, her mouth to his cheek, and then his forehead and nose, as if she couldn't force herself to move away this time.

He felt her sigh gently against his skin and step away, but before he could utter a word about having to stop, she took his hand.

'Come with me.'

She led him to the study, where he stood by the window set into a wall of ancient maps of shipping routes. People on the port bustled about with bags and trolleys while Adrienne, still smelling like an intoxicating floral bouquet he probably should be trying much harder not to touch, set up a presentation. She seemed nervous. Was it about her work? Or were the afternoon's events and that last kiss making her angsty? Probably all of the above.

He could have kicked himself—what had he literally just told Benni? This was getting out of control.

But he'd been just as worried about her out there. Adrienne had looked as if she'd had the soul sucked right out of her, searching the beach for him and that little girl. He'd seen the terror in her eyes—proof that she cared for him if ever he'd needed it. But now here she was, back in her fortress, fixated, agitated, insistent that whatever she'd been hiding had to be shared with him *now*.

Why now? he kept wondering, but he wasn't about to deny her a listening ear. This was why she was here, after all. Doing all she could to become the best doctor she could be—not just for him and their patients, but for the entire Kingdom of Lisri. Even if she'd become someone's bored, unsatisfied wife at the same time, he thought begrudgingly, wishing the taste of her wasn't so damn addictive.

They were due to sail to Capri at sunset. His father and his guests had been equally enthralled and horrified when they'd arrived on board and heard what had happened to Emma. Especially Allegra.

Allegra Aphelion, a specialist at the medical advisory board, was a tall, slender woman of French/Swiss descent, dressed as if to represent the best of middle-aged corporate conditioning. She had been beyond impressed to learn that Franco had brought a child back from the brink before the paramedics could reach them.

'You saved her life!'

'It's what we aim for every day in our line of work, Mrs Aphelion,' he'd replied.

The advisory board weren't his favourite bunch of bureaucrats, but perhaps Allegra had no idea of the situation they were in. There were hundreds of people behind the scenes of a new drug trial, drowning in paperwork and legalities. Maybe she had no real clue about the number of lives that depended on them all working together.

He knew if he had too many cocktails, he might spill his thoughts on it all, so he'd politely refused them all so far. As had Adrienne.

'OK, I'm ready,' Adrienne said behind him now. She had hooked up her laptop to the projector, and what he saw on the screen made him do a double-take.

'That's *you*,' he said pointlessly, thrown by

what he was looking at—a photo of Adrienne
in a white coat with her pink stethoscope, and
a gold and red swirling logo above her reading
Survive&Thrive. 'What is this?'

'I hope you don't mind that I haven't shown it
to you till now. You seemed to be so concerned
about protecting my privacy, and I appreciate
that, but this is too important. I didn't want you
to stop me before I was ready. I want to do this.'

'Adrienne…'

'This is part of the new Marx-Balthus Foundation,' she explained, standing behind the desk.

Tendrils of her hair framed her blue eyes, and
the fierce determination and pride in them struck
him silent. The boat started juddering beneath
them, but she didn't falter.

'I've had a team working on it for a while now.
They're based in Lisri. We have a website and
an app, so far. It tells a story of hope, based on
your work with the cancer patients and survivors
who took part in the trial. It offers them a place
to connect.'

Franco sank to the leather seat by the window, his mouth agape over the spinning globe
on the table.

What the hell…?

'I spoke to them all, Franco. All their stories
are here—all the ways they were helped and how
they're now thriving. I spoke to their families too.
And there are links to new medical trials on the

go—ones that are still in development—and incentives to push things forward, how and where to start collectively raising our voices…'

'How did you even come up with this?' His stomach was churning with all the emotions he had no clue how to put into words. 'You did all this by yourself?'

'I was merely being prudent,' she said. 'Trying something different to break the deadlock. I thought if we couldn't reach the medical advisory board by conventional means… There's always a back door, right? We can reach people like this instead. Look.'

She brought up images one by one. The website was a medley of heartfelt stories told from the mouths of the patients for a change, instead of doctors and scientists.

There was Bianca. The girl was still cancer-free, after just half the predicted chemo cycles for her cancer. And Martijn from the Netherlands, just eight when he'd been on the trial, also cured. He'd gone on to become a swimming champion, and now held counselling groups at his hospital for other kids with cancer. There was Felicity, a striking blonde woman who'd been devastated by breast cancer in her late twenties. She was now cancer-free, thanks to her participation in the trial. She'd won a scholarship for a PhD in Natural Science and was the very definition of thriving.

The pictures kept coming. The stories were heart-wrenching—they'd tug at anyone's heart, he knew—but each one ended on a high. He and his team had done a lot of good with these people, and this was the proof. Adrienne had brought it all together—all of it.

At the end of each deeply personal story was a pre-designed social media post, and a plea to contact local representatives who might help push for more important research and medical trials—predominantly the one that was currently blocked.

'So that's why you wanted to be here this weekend so badly,' he said, remembering how she'd called Allegra the key.

It was still a long shot, but how could anyone fail to be moved by this? It was at least worth a try. It was creative, compassionate, empathetic, empowering, and leagues beyond anything all the medical teams he surrounded himself with had ever come up with.

'If we happen to show it to Allegra this weekend she might just take it on board,' he said. 'She'll talk about it with us, at least, and then hopefully talk to other people on the board.'

'That's what I was thinking.'

'You're amazing.' He sank back in his chair again, his mind spinning. His foul mood had been squeezed right out of him, to be replaced with sheer wonder. 'And you've put your name all over this. How did you keep it a secret?'

'Very strict confidentiality agreements,' she told him. 'But I can lift them any time I like. There's an embargo on the press release, but it can all be announced tomorrow morning if I say so. Your team will need to be briefed, of course, but we can easily align...'

'I wish you hadn't felt like this was something you had to do in secret.' He sprang from the chair, but stopped short of sweeping her off her feet. His breath caught as she stood there, frozen inches from him. Waiting. 'Maybe I've been a little over-protective of you.'

Like your family, he realised suddenly, ashamed of treating her the same way as them when she was clearly a force to be reckoned with.

This time he did reach for her, and swept a hand behind her head, urging her lips to his. He wanted to claim more than her mouth right now—more than he had this afternoon, when she'd turned her back on him and that woman on the beach who'd clamoured for his attention like a puppy dog. It had turned him on, knowing she'd been looking.

'You did the right thing, not involving me in this,' he said instead, reining himself in and crossing to the laptop, where he studied the Survive&Thrive logo up close. 'It needed your personal touch. Your heart and soul. It's all here. I would have ruined it—made it all scientific and medical—but you...'

'It's still those things. It's just personal too. And, actually, you were my inspiration,' she said.

Behind him he heard her exhale, like a rush of fire leaving her body. She knew they had to stop surrendering to their impulses. Especially here. He was already too involved than was safe for his own heart. And now this.

'Do you think it will convince them?'

'Do you think what will convince who?'

Marco Perretta poked his grey head around the door and narrowed his eyes at them.

'What are you two doing, hiding out down here?'

'He should see it,' Franco told her. 'If you want the Perretta Institute to back this, that is?'

Adrienne glanced between them, as if weighing up whether or not to share it with someone else and his throat itched. She hadn't directly said she wanted his input. She'd done this all on her own, to her credit. She certainly didn't need them to back her. Not as far as the financials were involved.

To his relief, Adrienne beckoned his father closer and pulled up a seat for him in front of the projector. Then she stood in front of them both, ready for business.

'Let me run through my objectives for you, Mr Perretta.'

CHAPTER NINETEEN

ADRIENNE'S PRESS TEAM wanted to ask her a million things, and by eight a.m. she was starting to regret that she was on a yacht between islands on the Amalfi Coast. Still, timing had never been her speciality. And at least they had someone from the medical board here, in person, to watch it all play out.

She fetched a croissant from a fresh plate on the bar by the pool and accepted a coffee in a silver-crested cup. She was the first on deck, and today felt good already.

She and Franco had been up late, huddled in the study, going over the details of what would be announced by the press and how the Perretta Institute would correspond in alignment. They hadn't had a chance to be alone.

Finally Marco had called Franco to the entertainment hall for their customary midnight nightcap and she'd taken herself to bed, and fallen asleep the second her head hit the pillow. At least falling asleep exhausted was better than spending all night thinking about *him* sleeping in the stateroom opposite her, and wishing she could go to him.

This was about something else now, she reminded herself, adjusting her sunglasses and tying the robe around her swimsuit.

Her mother was the first to call, just as she'd settled on a lounger, and Adrienne allowed a small shiver of pride and anticipation to swirl through her with the caffeine as the Queen chattered on profusely about how proud she was. The embargo had been lifted on Survive&Thrive. And with her name attached to it, it was getting attention very fast.

'What does Papa think?' She had to ask.

Her mother paused, as if searching for the right words. 'He did say he'd like to meet this Dr Perretta one day. He's aware of the impression he seems to have made on you. Why don't you bring him to the polo?'

Adrienne's heart lodged in her throat. 'He's not the kind of man Papa would approve of.'

The Queen fell silent.

'But the kind of man he approves of has never been the kind of man for me. You know that, don't you, Mother?' Adrienne continued. She realised her heart was thrumming. 'I'll be a member of the royal family *and* a doctor, Mother. I'll do everything that's expected of me and more. But I've told you before: I won't marry any man I don't love.'

'Are you telling me you love this man?'

Adrienne balked. 'I… No, of course not. It's

just that he and I have work to do. I don't want
Papa to come between us, or put a spanner in the
works for any reason.'

Still more silence.

Adrienne lost her appetite on the spot. Of
course she wasn't telling her mother the whole
truth, even though she'd probably read between
the lines of her letters. But surprisingly, a huge
leaden weight seemed to drift from her shoulders
and she dared to exhale deeply. She might as well
tell her everything now—God knew she'd been
bottling it up.

She walked to the bow, cast her eyes over the
sea and the boats with their sails jutting like shark
fins in the distance. Then, in a hushed voice, she
told her mother how she really felt about Franco.
About how their lives were vastly different, how
his future didn't align with hers and how it killed
her. How Franco didn't want the never-ending
circus that was her life, but how he'd shown her
lately that sticking to her principles and staying
single, instead of marrying someone for the sake
of the throne, was simply what she had to do.

She would have sworn her mother took it on
board, but then came her departing warning.

'My darling, just take care of yourself. I'm not
going to tell you what to do at your age, but…
why don't you just meet the Baron?'

And there she goes again.

Adrienne swiped at her face, pursing her lips.

'There is no law saying I have to marry a member of the aristocracy or another royal, Mother, only an archaic tradition,' she said tightly. 'And Papa would do well to remember that—both of you would—if I'm to continue our honoured legacy. I don't want to be a monarch who lies, Mother, not about my own worth, and not about my own heart's desires. What kind of role model would that make me?'

Adrienne was shaking; she had never said anything of the sort to either of her parents. But she'd summoned the strength Franco had given her out in that hot pool when he'd challenged her. It was high time she fought back and addressed some home truths.

'Buongiorno, sole.'

Franco's whisper in her ear made her jump, just as she was hanging up. Her conversation with her mother was unresolved, but she'd call again in a few days...talk to Papa if she really had to.

She spun round and swallowed back an anxious flutter—first at the thought of telling Papa what she'd just told her mother, then at seeing Franco.

He looked even more handsome than yesterday, in another pair of low-slung shorts and a navy shirt, worn open. His taut abdominals gleamed in the morning sun and made her look twice, and then stifle a moan as he dropped to a deckchair and pulled out his phone.

'It's everywhere already,' he said as she stood over him.

He stopped scrolling through the web browser to eye her from head to toe in the swimsuit, then dragged another chair to his side for her, as if they were honeymooners or something, waking up to look at their wedding photos.

God, her imagination around this guy...

He still had a faint pillow crease on one fore-arm and across one cheek, and she imagined him some fifteen minutes earlier, sound asleep with no clothes on, just feet from her suite. The sooner they got off this boat, where she was already far too tempted by him, the better.

'"Princess Adrienne Marx-Balthus of Lisri garners support for new cancer drug trial",' he read aloud, as a deckhand brought him coffee. '"Revolutionary new connections for cancer patients..." "The Princess with a promise..." These headlines... Adrienne, everyone's talk-ing about it.'

She flushed at the look of pure awe on his face. 'Lisri's *Evening News* called the press office,' she told him. 'They want some of the kids to do a TV piece. You and me too.'

'You and me, huh?'

His expression grew serious, and a smile played on his perfect lips. In spite of her appre-hension about the whole thing, she felt a flock of excited butterflies take flight in her belly, fol-

lowed quickly by a twinge of nerves. Everything
hinged on their meeting with Allegra. Franco and
his father had had no luck using conventional
means so far—now it was up to her.

No one had put any pressure on her, but for
once she was putting it on herself and enjoying
it. She'd never been so fired up and flustered at
the same time.

Hours later they were all sitting on a flower-
lined terrace at the foot of Punta Carena Light-
house. Essentially it was a terrace above the
sea, overlooking a gorgeous cove. The seafood
lunch was perfect, but every time Allegra looked
her way Adrienne waited for her to bring up
Survive&Thrive. She knew she couldn't be the
first to mention it—the news would have spread
on its own.

Before leaving the yacht, Franco and his prin-
ciple investigator had given Allegra a presentation on the status of another current trial, to
which Allegra had listened intently and quietly.
No one had been looking at their phones. Which
had given the news more time to circulate.

Thankfully it wasn't long before two men from
the Perretta biotechnology lab in Florence started
whispering, then looking at her. She put down
her fork.

'What is this?' one of them asked, and her
heart sped up as she took the man's phone.

Survive&Thrive was all over it. She could feel Allegra watching her, too, now.

'Survive&Thrive—It means going beyond your comfort zone. And also, using your courage to help the people around you.'

'That's Adrienne,' Franco said, and pride swirled in his eyes, hypnotising her for a second.

Allegra's phone rang.

Under the table, he knocked his knee against hers and she tried not to feel the zing of desire for him creep along her inner thighs.

'I'm getting hundreds of calls about this—and emails,' Allegra said, scrolling through her phone without answering it and looking between them in amusement. 'They know I'm here with you and they all want the scoop.' Her eyebrows furrowed as she read something else, then turned to her, shaking her head. 'This is quite an endeavour, Princess Adrienne, how did you find the time?'

'Well, to be quite honest, Allegra, I don't really know,' Adrienne answered truthfully, and a nervous laugh escaped her lips before she could stop it.

'I don't know what to say.' Allegra put her phone down on the table. 'I'm humbled, honestly, and I can only apologise for all the delays you and the institute have experienced so far, trying to push your trial through. All my CTAs are telling me to chase the board. They're getting calls already.'

'It's not your fault,' Adrienne said. 'But that was what we kind of hoped would happen.'

Allegra nodded, fighting a smile. 'I will do everything I can,' she said.

Franco and Marco let out a joint sigh of relief, and just hearing it made Adrienne reach for Allegra's hands. 'Thank you,' she said, 'from the bottom of my heart.' Allegra looked somewhat embarrassed for a second. 'We need more public awareness of the good these new treatments can do. We need all the support we can get.'

She couldn't help thinking of Rosita, waiting for another bout of chemo, and Candice, waiting for her hair to fall out when it didn't necessarily have to.

Cancer had a way of creeping into everyone's life at some point—if not directly, then by way of someone else. Furious determination flooded her veins. For her, cancer of every kind had merged into one huge iniquitous dragon she wanted nothing more but to slay, piece by piece, no matter how long it took.

Franco was quiet at her side, taking it all in, ignoring his own vibrating phone. Her knee was still buzzing from where his had been pressed against it. He was with her on this. Even if it was as far as they ever went he was her partner in this mission, and for that, at least, she was satisfied.

Liar. You want him. More than just his kisses. Allegra was wiping her eyes behind the sunglasses she'd chosen to hide behind for a moment. It was an emotional moment for everyone, it seemed. 'I give you my word I'll do what I can to get your trial moving. All your hard work won't be for nothing, Princess.'

CHAPTER TWENTY

FRANCO KNOCKED ON the door at ten p.m. and Adrienne answered with a radiant smile. She'd been locked away in the study fielding calls since they'd returned from lunch. Suddenly she was more in demand than ever, but she didn't look unhappy about it.

'Everything's coming together,' she said, stifling a yawn and rubbing her eyes.

She was clearly as exhausted as he was. He should say goodnight and retire, and he knew it. He'd been bursting with pride over her achievements all day—even more so after seeing Allegra's reaction—but as he'd scrolled through the news announcements he'd been hit with the fact that being linked to her on this project was bound to come with all kinds of unwanted attention—more than usual.

She rested her head on her hand against the door frame. 'When we get back to Naples tomorrow I have a couple of interviews to do, but then my team will take over. Don't worry, it won't affect my regular work, but I do have a lot of studying to catch up on.'

'I'm sure we can work out an extension for you,' he told her, letting his eyes run over her outfit—a lilac dress that emphasised her slim hips and full, round breasts. He was so tired it was all he could do to force his eyes away.

'An extension? Wouldn't that be special treatment?' She smiled.

He cleared his throat, forcing his hand not to adjust the strap of her dress as it drifted down over her shoulder.

'I guess it would, but you deserve it.'

He would not ruin her moment by asking if the royal family were dubious in any way about him being at her side in her latest venture. It was certainly bringing attention to her role at the institute already, as well as to him. News travelled incredibly fast—especially when a member of Lisri's royal family was involved. The Perretta Foundation had been flooded with calls all day.

'Big day,' he said, and she nodded, looking slightly awkward.

His words seemed to hang in the salty air, and for a second he considered saying goodnight, just as he'd planned.

'Get your swimsuit on,' he said instead, realising he'd only lie there imagining her in the next cabin.

'What?'

'I have something to show you. Meet me on deck.'

* * *

The grotto was just one of several sea caves around the island. Tonight, as he rowed the small boat from the yacht, the bioluminescence created a brilliant blue light that made the cave look alive.

Above them, the yellow half-moon lit Adrienne as she trailed a finger over the side of the small boat into the water, her hair loose around her shoulders. His thoughts were still crashing over him like waves, even though he'd tried to calm them down. The stakes would be higher than ever now. Her medical role would be under scrutiny along with his. Her family would be watching her even more closely, and more noble suitors would be rolled out. There was no doubt about it.

He was more than happy to be her partner in this new business venture, but one newspaper had already caused a stir online this afternoon, hinting that one day he might be trying to rule the nation alongside her, with no experience and no background, and no blue blood at all.

It was bothering him more than he cared to admit.

'Can we really swim in there?' she asked, pulling him from his thoughts.

The yawning mouth of the cave was an open invitation to a glistening blue-tinted wonderland. There was no one else around.

'We can in this one,' he said. 'When the tide is right.'

It was right tonight. He anchored the boat at the mouth of the cave and stood, kicked off his shirt and shoes. Adrienne's eyes trailed across his bare torso nervously, like a mouse that had been lured to some kind of trap and was considering whether or not to try and take the cheese.

'You don't have to swim,' he heard himself say. 'But I am.'

With that he dived into the cool, càlm water, and in three seconds flat she was carving through the water behind him, swimming right into the cave.

He watched her tread water, spinning circles in the entrance. The bioluminescence glowed beneath her and swirled around her in a dream-like soup.

'It's like a movie set,' she breathed, floating onto her back.

Her silhouette against every shade of blue was worth filming without doubt, he thought, but it was just them here. No cameras. No one to see them at all. He could look, but he still shouldn't touch. It was glaringly apparent how different their lives were; they were on different trajectories.

His heart was not a toy for the media to play with.

She asked for a story about the cave, so he

flipped onto his back beside her and told her about the Emperor's private swimming pool. This very place. It had once been elaborately decorated inside—a kind of temple in the ocean, in honour of the sea nymphs. Long ago, no one had known what made it glow. They'd thought it was magic.

'It *is* magic,' she breathed from where she was floating beside him.

Her shoulder knocked his as a wave swept in from a passing boat outside, and she reached for his hand.

'It's just a boat,' he told her, feeling her warm fingers tighten in his. 'I thought you were an expert sailor?'

'I am.'

She pulled her hand back quickly, and he tried not to notice how just one touch had, yet again, sent his heartbeat straight to his manhood.

'This is all just so different. Everything about this place. If my family could see me now...'

'What would they say?' He had to ask her now she'd brought it up. 'Have you heard from them?'

She kept her eyes on the roof of the cave. 'My mother is very proud of me. I haven't heard from my father yet, but I don't care what he thinks.'

'Yes, you do.'

She sighed. 'You're right. I do.'

'He wouldn't try and bring you home, would he? Now that you're involved in a different cause?'

'A cause that's not to do with marrying myself off to the nearest suitable man, you mean?'

He chewed on his cheek. He couldn't even find the notion funny. 'A cause that involves you being seen alongside someone who's not of blue blood.'

Adrienne turned to him. 'I know the media are already speculating that we might be more to each other than colleagues. That's just what they do. I'm sorry.'

'It's not your fault,' he said truthfully.

'But I couldn't have done this without you. You give me reasons and avenues to push into and prove myself.'

She righted herself in the water, met his eyes an inch above the rippling blue hues. Her whole face glowed turquoise, her lips and eyelashes dripping.

'Is it wrong that I want you?' she whispered suddenly, and closed the gap between them. 'I know I shouldn't.'

'You're right...you shouldn't,' he heard himself say, as the bulge in his shorts screamed for attention.

He swallowed. This was the Crown Princess of Lisri, putty in his hands. Or maybe it was the other way round. He was the putty...

Ducking beneath the water, he swam away from her, trying to cool the heated blood throbbing through every inch of him. He came up three feet away to find her floating on her back again, sucking the air from the cave in huge, needy lung-fuls, eyes closed.

'I'm not what you want?'

Her voice was small, and he hated what he was doing—to both of them.

'Adrienne, that's not it.'

Damn this. How was he supposed to forget what they'd already done? He could deny it all he liked, but he hadn't wanted anyone like this since Luci—and never as badly.

The Princess of Lisri…his for the taking. Certain responsibilities came with that…they both knew it. But he was so hard for her already. Blue blood, blue eyes imploring—how could he refuse her?

Excitement pounded and drummed in her veins as Franco's green eyes seemed to devour her. She let her gaze rake over his broad shoulders, bulging pectoral muscles and rippling abs.

'Make love to me,' she heard herself say, swimming up close to him again. 'I'm protected against pregnancy.'

Her words seemed to echo around the cave, and for a moment he caressed her face with a palm, eyes harrowed and tortured. It made her want him more, and without thinking another second she pressed her mouth to his, till they were kissing furiously, passionately, making for the line of rocks at the edge of the cave.

God, you're amazing, she wanted to say.

Every muscle was hard as he drew her closer with thick, heavy arms, and she thought he'd be able to wrestle a sea monster to the ocean floor if he wanted. Her hands slid like water over his shoulders, up and down his biceps, and all the while she kissed him, tracing the lines of his body, committing them to memory. She let her fingers tangle in his hair and trail downwards, to his shorts...

'*Adrienne...*'

His gaze locked to hers as his hands found their way to her hips. He was waiting to see what she would do, leaving it up to her. She wasn't going to wait now that she'd started. The water defined each line on his body as he swam with her, guiding her to a long, flat rock the right size for them to rest on. Or do whatever the hell they wanted on.

She slid a hand into his shorts, finding him so hard for her she moaned, and the need to explore more of him took over her entire thought process.

Franco's mouth fell open. His chest seemed to expand before her as he took in a huge lungful of the salty air. She hooked a finger into the waistband of his shorts, teased him towards her, hardly believing how daring she was, how desirous she was for him at her core.

He was still holding his breath as she drew his shorts down, and she watched his biceps flex as he pulled them off and tossed them to the rocks, finally letting his breath out and crashing his mouth to hers again. In seconds her bikini was on top of them, making a wet pile next to their naked bodies.

He drew her against him by her hips, his back to the rock, and she found her hands caressing his tight backside, urging him closer. He was so hard for her—huge, in fact—and she heard herself gasp as he deftly pulled himself onto the rock, revealing the full extent of his manhood, every glistening inch of his rock-hard body. She wanted all of it.

He lifted her easily onto the rock beside him, and before she could touch him again he brought both his palms to her face and pressed his hungry lips to hers, kissed her till she was dizzy. As his palms slid expertly over the dripping curves of her skin she swooned audibly, till she found herself sitting astride him, naked before him.

Her knees quaked as he continued to kiss her and she slid her hand between them, along and up the straining length of him till he was making sounds she'd never heard…music to her ears. Pleasing him, it emerged, was her new favourite thing. She wouldn't allow herself to think about how she shouldn't be doing this…that she might regret it later. That *he* might.

Franco's own fingers were anything but idle. She took his lower lip in her teeth and grasped his thickness as they found her sweetest spot, revelling at the look on his face when she opened her eyes. Suddenly, neither of them could wait any more. He rolled her expertly onto her back, protecting her head from the rock with his hand, and slid inside her. With every thrust she felt herself falling deeper into him; it was futile trying to think of anything else.

This was the moment she'd been waiting for, and it was better than she ever could have imagined.

CHAPTER TWENTY-ONE

Two weeks went past in a flash for Adrienne. The phone never seemed to stop, and she had her work cut out, making time for interviews about Survive&Thrive on top of her regular duties at the cancer institute.

'You look tired, Princess,' Rosita observed when she poked her head into her room one morning.

Rosita was hooked up to fluids and looked pale. Her cancer treatment plan was intense. Every time Adrienne saw her she yearned for something more positive to report regarding a place on the soon-to-be revived trial, but there was still no word from the medical advisory board. Although there was more pressure on them to get it moving than ever.

The people she'd interviewed had all been re-interviewed separately by various news outlets. The app had over half a million downloads already. All proceeds had gone straight to the Perretta Institute. It was now something of a buzzword on the medical scene…not that any of it had moved her father any closer to admitting he was proud of her.

He'd said very little, and she wondered if he was debating how to berate her for appearing so publicly with Franco Perretta in a cause that might lead her further from her royal duties than he preferred.

Not that she needed his approval, of course. But her pride and happiness over the project was overshadowed somewhat by the feeling that all was not well in the kingdom. Nor with Franco.

No, she would not be led back down that path, she reprimanded herself.

But how could she not?

They'd given in to their desires and it had been the most incredible sexual encounter of her life—but he'd been keeping away from her ever since, outside of the institute, and she had a feeling that this intense invasion of his privacy was getting to him. She felt awful, knowing that he was getting papped everywhere he went because of her.

'How's the latest round treating you?' she asked her patient now. She knew Rosita's chemo was already taking its toll, and this time she'd had to spend even longer as an in-patient.

'This is my third day...' Rosita sighed, pressing her raven-haired head to the pillows propped up at her back. The room was filled with vases of flowers. The TV on the wall flickered with no sound. 'At least I made it past Chapter Three this time.'

She held up the copy of *Great Expectations*

that Franco had lent her. He'd insisted she should finish it. Adrienne smiled, even though the sight of it made her wonder where he was—still out entertaining a certain diet specialist named Nicolette de Luca, who was about to give a lecture in the hall with him?

'That's when it starts getting good,' she said, trying not to sound distracted.

'I've been on Survive&Thrive again,' Rosita said now. 'I contacted a girl in Austria, younger than me. She just got diagnosed with Ewing's sarcoma. She's written to the medical board every day about the trial, like my parents have. Do you think they're even reading the emails?'

Her eyes looked round and hopeful, and Adrienne felt a lump in her throat instantly. A downside to all the attention around the trial, through the website and the app, was that the people who weren't getting the help they needed were hearing about it. Not that ignorance had been blissful for them to begin with. Allegra had promised to help, but they couldn't really rely on one insider—they all knew that.

It felt as if some kind of clock was ticking.

What if her grand plan didn't actually work?

What if she'd dragged Franco into the limelight and encouraged all this relentless tongue-wagging about them both for nothing?

'There are other ways for you to get better,' she said, trying to sound cheerful in spite of herself.

She squeezed the young girl's hand, wishing her thoughts weren't always such a tornado.

Franco himself stuck his head around the door. 'What are you two gossiping about?'

Her pulse soared. So he was back.

'Rosita has a massage soon.'

She was trying to sound impervious to his presence, but probably failing. She hadn't seen him now for three days. He'd been on Capri with a science research team. Then Nicolette de Luca had invited him to discuss the results of her study on the treatment of advanced cancer by diet therapy.

'Ah, you're getting into it.' Franco strode to her side and took the book from Rosita's hand. He ran a thumb over the embossed cover and threw a look her way. 'Charles Dickens…what a guy…' He put the book back down. 'Of course it's really a study on class and society.'

'I know,' Rosita said, and her eyes danced between them with interest.

Adrienne did her best to look busy, tucking in a blanket that didn't need to be tucked in at all. She wanted to apologise for bringing unwelcome speculation by strangers into his life, but every time she tried it was as if she was underlining another reason for him not to come any closer, and there was enough distance between them already. She'd read more than one piece of trash that accused him of trying to line himself up for his place as her husband. The thought of him seeing it made her cringe. He was such a private guy; this was probably a total nightmare for him.

'If you'll excuse me, ladies? Some people over on the radiation ward have "great expectations" for my afternoon. I'll see you shortly for the lecture, Dr Balthus?'

'I wouldn't miss it,' she answered before Franco strode from the room.

Rosita was grinning now, her clever eyes seeing deeper into Adrienne than she cared to show. 'Is something really going on with you and the hot doc? Like all the articles are saying?'

'Don't be silly,' Adrienne said lightly, willing her heart to slow down as the weight of it all came crashing back down onto her shoulders. 'I'll have Irina come back in…'

'Nicolette de Luca was kind enough to let me stay on the premises in Capri, where her patients are free to explore the most beautiful grounds. I've never seen such lush vegetable gardens… Even I might be going vegan after this.'

Adrienne sank a little lower in her seat in the study hall. Franco was doing his thing on stage, being as charismatic and charming as only he knew how. Even when the surgeon Ansell shuffled into the seat next to her, she couldn't keep her eyes off Franco.

The lecture was actually fascinating. The Perretta Institute was getting behind a grant for Nicolette de Luca's latest research programme, and its results on cancer-fighting foods, which they were being walked through now, were promising.

Nicolette's willowy figure was the picture of elegance in an open white coat, with her high, full breasts pert in a tight white shirt. She wore her bright red hair loose and spoke Italian with a refined accent.

And she was standing a little too close to Franco.

Jealousy was a wicked beast. Adrienne could picture the two of them these last three nights, drinking herbal tea, working late by candlelight... Franco would have been wooed by the dietician, eating her delicious fruits, maybe allowing himself to release some of the pent-up energy Adrienne had left him with after their one incredible, wet, hot night together that no one must know about—ever.

She'd given in to her burning, raging need to feel him inside her, and she'd have to live with the lack of that glorious experience for ever.

Wondering about it had almost been better. Now she knew exactly what she'd be missing when he moved on with someone more suitable for him than her. She should try to forget the rush of those salty kisses, the way his skin had glistened in that glowing cave, how powerful she'd felt, how *seen* and worshipped by him, and...

'That's absolutely right, Nicolette. Results show that polyphenols possess anti-cancer and tumour-fighting properties…'

Was he flirting with Nicolette to distract the press from the subject of the two of them, seeing as he loathed being in the public eye even more than Adrienne did? She wouldn't blame him. He hadn't asked to have his family history compared to that of every aristocrat now climbing out of the woodwork to try and set up a meeting with her. And it was up to her to do something about it.

'How are you doing, Adrienne?' Ansell nudged her slightly, so softly she barely felt it, and she remembered he'd slid in next to her.

'Yes, great…' she said, distracted.

There was no escaping this. She had to talk to her family—open up and be honest. She had to drive it home that she was her own person, paving her own future, with or without a man at her side.

'Dr Perretta, you should know an apple a day keeps the doctor away—but have you heard about what urolithins in walnuts can do? Our studies have found that these compounds, which bind to oestrogen receptors, may play a role in preventing breast cancer.'

Oh, Nicolette, you're good.

'So, I was wondering if you were busy on Friday…' Ansell's voice was in her ear now. He was asking her out again.

'Hmmm?' she managed, barely hearing him.

They were both just doing their job, Franco and Nicolette, and Franco was a free man. His kisses had not been promises, and their lovemaking, while it had been the best of her life, hadn't changed her situation, or his stance against being the centre of any kind of scandal.

It was up to her to turn things around—if not for herself, then for all future generations of women in Lisri.

'Your phone's vibrating.'

Ansell again.

'Oh, yes…thanks.'

She was about to turn it off when she saw it was a message for her from Reception.

Someone is here to see you.

Her heart jolted.

Something must be wrong. People didn't just show up unannounced—not for her, anyway. She had a schedule.

As quickly as she could, she squeezed through the rows towards the exit.

CHAPTER TWENTY-TWO

NICOLETTE DE LUCA WAS MAKING quite an impression on Rosita, telling her what she might try eating to help her feel less tired between chemo sessions. They were talking about horses now, comparing where they'd gone riding last summer, and the redhead kept shooting him looks, as if she was checking how impressed he was by her.

Franco rolled his eyes when her back was turned. Women who flirted so brazenly were almost always after one thing: one hot night with *Medical Heroes* magazine's Philanthropist of the Decade. These days he preferred those who wouldn't go near him at all—even if it left him hornier than a stag.

But it was better this way. The press were relentless, just as Adrienne had always said.

It wasn't that he minded his name being out there, attributed to *her* work—in fact, he was immensely proud of what she'd achieved—but being accused of being 'unsuitable' for her, simply because he wasn't an aristocrat…

He'd gone through enough torture, sympathy and gossip after losing Luci, thanks to keeping his grief and thoughts to himself. He didn't need his private life splashed in the world's press again. It made him cold to the bone, knowing that his every breath outside the institute was under scrutiny.

'Where is Dr Balthus?' Rosita asked him.

'I think she's in the Residents' Room,' he replied. 'She's busy.'

At least they'd both been busy...busy enough to justify keeping away from each other and keeping all temptation at bay.

With her website and the app a full success, Survive&Thrive was the talk of the institute—and most of Europe by now. It was all go. Over half a million downloads... New connections being made every minute... Hope delivered daily to people who needed it...

His phone rang.

Would it have taken off like this without her name behind it? Who cared? he thought. It didn't even matter. She'd been interviewed by everyone of any importance and, while he hadn't dared to say it aloud, he'd been expecting a phone call for days now.

'Excuse me,' he said to Nicolette, answering his phone at the same time. His heart was an ox, bashing his ribs under his lab coat. What if it *wasn't* what he'd been expecting...?

'It seems your Princess has caused a bit of a stir with this Survive&Thrive project,' said Nathan, chair of the medical advisory board. There was the sound chattering behind him, people talking excitedly. 'You'd better get your patient list together, Franco.'

Franco stopped short in the middle of the floor. 'Are you saying what I think you're saying?'

'Someone on the board has been fighting your case hard, and it seems we can finally approve the move from phase two to phase three within the month.'

Yes. Yes. Yes. Thank God.

Franco couldn't help it. He gave a loud whoop as he turned back to Nicolette, and Rosita laughed from the bed. 'The trial has got approval to move on,' he told them in jubilation.

'You're the first to know. We thought you'd want to tell Dr Balthus yourself,' Nathan said.

Franco told him, yes, of course, all the while raking his hand through his hair, picturing her face when he told her.

Nicolette spoke. 'Franco, do you want me to come with you?'

He realised he was headed for the door, his mind elsewhere. 'I have to go do and something—excuse me, ladies. I'll be right back,' he said, and left the room without her.

His indifference towards Nicolette was only making her try harder. She should have left an hour ago, but she'd said she wanted to meet Adrienne when she was free—and who didn't these days?

* * *

'Adrienne? I have some news.'

He hovered outside the door. She was being very quiet…maybe she had her headphones on. He considered for a second not telling her here at all. This warranted going somewhere special, with champagne… But, no, he wasn't doing things like that any more. Nothing that drew unwarranted attention to him as some potential wholly unsuitable suitor was not even an option. It was about the trial, not them.

'Adrienne?'

With a tentative hand he opened the door, expecting to find her there. All the chairs were empty, like the rest of the room. Frowning to himself, he remembered she'd left the lecture early. He assumed she'd come back here to push on with her studies.

He stood there for a minute, annoyed at how his brain was deconstructing her absence already. Not knowing where she was made him uneasy—which bothered him.

He pulled out his phone, annoyed again when his pulse quickened in anticipation of talking to her. It rang out, and then high-heeled footsteps in the corridor told him Nicolette had followed him.

'Franco? I forgot to tell you…there's a restaurant launch in Rione Sanita tonight. I have two tickets. It's vegan—your new favourite.'

She wasn't going to quit.

He forced a smile, crossing to one of the desks. Adrienne's laptop was there, closed. It wasn't like her not to take it with her.

'I think we should celebrate,' Nicolette said from the doorway, folding her arms and wriggling her eyebrows suggestively.

The old him would have buried himself in her to get his mind off Adrienne.

He watched her eye the brown carpet of the residents' room with a hint of disapproval, tossing her long red hair over her shoulder. 'This is not exactly fit for a princess,' she said with a sniff.

He bit back a smile. The Crown Princess hadn't turned her nose up. Adrienne had given the institute nothing but compliments, and done nothing but good since she'd arrived. She'd also helped him address a few things about his own life. She was a leader, someone to look up to…audacious, driven, and so damn beautiful, inside and out…

He tried her phone again.

Come on, pick up… Where are you, woman?

Dropping to a seat, he stared unseeingly at Nicolette as Adrienne's phone rang out. For a second he considered that maybe she'd actually flown home without telling him. She'd mentioned something about an annual polo match this weekend in Lisri. She wasn't going to go, though— she'd told the team so herself, said she was too busy. Had she changed her mind?

'Wow, what on earth…?' Nicolette trailed off

as Irina entered the room, her face obscured by the hugest bunch of flowers he'd ever seen.

'I think we should keep these in here for the Princess. They're taking over the entire reception desk,' Irina said, wrinkling her nose. Then she sneezed. 'Gosh, have you ever seen anything like it? They're giving me hay fever.'

'Who are they from?' he asked, instincts primed.

'He just showed up with them before he left with her,' she replied, lowering the bouquet carefully to the desk in front of him, burying Adrienne's laptop under sunflowers, roses, and giant purple trumpet-like calla lilies. 'Charming man.'

'Who was charming?'

The back of his neck felt too hot under his collar. Nicolette was admiring the flowers now, fondling the satin ribbon around the base of the bouquet.

He bristled, stood up from the chair. 'Irina, who did Adrienne leave with?'

Irina shrugged, running her fingers along the head of a snow-white teddy bear, nestled in the blooms. Both women looked as awed as if an original Da Vinci had been deposited on the desk, and he didn't get a good feeling.

'I'm sure she said he was a baron. He had a very long, important name.'

'Lucky girl.' Nicolette looked impressed—and envious.

Franco felt a kick like a soccer ball to his guts.

CHAPTER TWENTY-THREE

ADRIENNE SCOOPED THE kitten into her arms and dismissed Mirabel the second she got home. She didn't feel much like talking. In fact, she desperately needed her own company after a day like today.

On the balcony, staring at Vesuvius, she felt her ears still ringing from listening to Baron Vittorio La Rosa going on about his tour of Mozambique, and wherever it was he'd been after that—she'd zoned out on a lot of it.

How infuriating that he'd tracked her down and just shown up like that. But it wasn't as if she could have just brushed him off, with Irina swooning behind her. And it wasn't *his* fault he'd been pushed on her.

He'd assumed she didn't want to meet when she hadn't contacted him, but his parents had insisted he try. He'd been pretty honest about that, once they'd started talking. It had been all their idea for him to come to the institute with a huge bouquet of flowers. His family didn't believe the rumours about her and Franco… *'Because obviously he's not husband material.'*

His words had boiled her blood, fired her up even more.

The Baron had talked a lot about a former boarding school friend called Carlos, who he'd just got back in touch with. After maybe the twentieth time of hearing his name she'd wondered if the Baron might actually be gay, and not so secretly in love with Carlos. If that were the case...*wow*. Imagine the pressure on him to be something he wasn't—forced to knock on princesses' doors before being shut back in the closet.

'My own situation could be worse, right, kitten?' she said, stroking the creature's silky fur as she switched on her phone again.

It pinged with the expected multitude of messages, and she scrolled through for the important ones. Three missed calls from Franco not long after she'd left the building. Her heart soared.

She called him back.

No answer.

Jealousy consumed her like a dark cloud. Maybe he'd gone out with Nicolette de Luca. He had every right to, of course, but that didn't stop the furious butterflies flapping when she called again and he still didn't answer.

The next morning she was surprised to see someone had put the Baron's flowers in the residents' room, as well as a huge card addressed to her. Bright red balloons and the word *Congratulations* glittered on the front.

Dropping her bag to a chair, she flipped it open. The whole team had signed it.

Congratulations on your success with Survive&Thrive and for helping to get the trial approved!

What...?

'Well done, Princess... I mean, Adrienne.'

Irina's voice in the doorway made her spin around.

'When did you find out?' she asked, propping up the card against the ridiculous bouquet and grabbing her white coat from the back of a chair. This was monumental—and she'd had no idea. Why had no one left her a message about this?

'Yesterday...late afternoon. Right after you left with the Baron. Franco was trying to get hold of you. I think he wanted to tell you himself...'

'He didn't call me back,' she said, missing a button on her coat.

Her head was spinning.

She found him after her rounds, before she was due to attend a radiation session. He didn't look too pleased to see her when she caught him exiting the consultation room.

'There you are,' she said, on edge immediately. 'Where have you been?'

'Busy,' he said curtly, making for the revolving door. 'Like you, I assume.'

She caught his arm in the corridor and couldn't help the grin taking over her face. 'Franco, the trial got approved!'

'I know,' he said bluntly. Then he straightened up. 'I called to tell you that yesterday.'

'I was out. I tried to call you back. This is so fantastic! We should talk… I want to stay involved.'

'We'll schedule a team meeting.'

His eyes narrowed at her, then moved to the floor. Her chest felt tight. He was angry with her. Maybe he'd seen the Baron's flowers. Who was she kidding? You could see them from the moon.

She cast her eyes around the corridor, then ushered him into an empty treatment room, closing the door behind them.

'Is this because of the flowers?' she said. 'Because I went for a coffee with the Baron?'

Franco made a thing of checking the clipboard he was holding. 'It's none of my business who you date, Adrienne.'

His coldness sent a chill through her veins. 'Franco, it wasn't a date. I just had to…'

'Regarding this trial… I assume you'd like to help reach out to potential patients?' He flipped through the papers on his clipboard, refusing to meet her eyes. 'Rosita and her parents have been informed. We can take two hundred people from all over Europe. And we'll start the first treatments at the institute next Friday.'

Oh, God. He's gone full doctor mentor on me. One hundred per cent colleague.

'I'd be happy to help, however you need me to,' she managed as her heart skidded and cracked. His eyes held none of the passion or sparkle he usually reserved for their encounters—not even now, after all his hard work had finally paid off.

'Franco, please don't be like this.'

'Adrienne. I have a life to get on with—as do you. Now, if you'll excuse me—?'

The ringing of his phone cut him off. Tutting, he whipped it from his pocket, and she watched his green eyes widen in surprise at the screen.

'What is it?' she asked, vice-like fear turning her voice tight.

Then her own phone went off.

All the breath left her lungs when she saw the screen. *Oh, no.*

There she was in her swimsuit, right next to Franco, wet, bedraggled, looking undeniably like more than colleagues. It was the photo that man had taken on the beach after they'd rescued little Emma—the one she had all but forgotten about.

He'd caught the exact moment Franco had walked up to her on the rocks and checked that she was OK. His big hands were frozen in motion, cradling her cheeks. Her eyes were gazing up at him in a way that spoke more than a thousand words about her feelings.

'I guess you got sent the same thing,' Franco said, letting out a harangued sigh. 'He must have waited for the right price…which they've given him now the drug trial has been approved because of you.'

Every breath felt tougher than the last. She felt as if the small white room was whirring around her.

This can't be happening.

Mortified, she sank into a chair by the wall. 'Someone from the royal court at Lisri sent it to me,' she said, trembling as reality hit her. 'Which means my parents have seen it.'

Franco's jaw was ticking. His face looked beyond enraged, the skin pinched around flared nostrils. She'd never seen him look like this. She'd humiliated him, just as she'd feared. Being at her side was causing him nothing but pain. To the world, this was confirmation of the rumours, and now he'd be badgered to death.

Her phone rang again. Someone at the royal court was calling her now.

Helplessly, she answered. Papa. The Prince Consort himself was on the end of the line. He wanted her home immediately.

She reminded him he couldn't summon her anywhere—that she wasn't attending the polo this weekend, nor the masquerade ball that followed it every year, that she had work to do at the cancer institute, and for Survive&Thrive.

But he wasn't having any of it. She was going to have to explain herself—issue a statement, which they'd have to construct together, in person, along with the Lisri media. Why had she gone out in a swimsuit, looking as if she was living some cheap Italian holiday romance?

'We'd just saved someone's life, Papa,' she reminded him.

'Do you know how this looks, Adrienne? I appreciate the work you and the doctor are doing is important, but so are we—so is your family name. You're embarrassing the royal family. We sent you there in good faith!'

He went on and on and on, and she wondered where the hell her mother was as she watched Franco by the window, shoulders held stiff, his face like thunder. She wanted to shout at the man who'd only ever half raised her, compared to his wife, her mother, the ever-loving Queen.

You don't care about me at all! You're just furious that none of your blue-blooded suitors will want anything to do with me if they see this!

But that wasn't a conversation she should start on the phone. She was going to have to stand her ground in person if she was going to make them listen to her once and for all.

'I have to go back to Lisri,' she told Franco when she'd hung up.

'I think you probably should,' he replied coolly, and strode from the room.

She sat there for a while, staring unseeingly at the walls, her thoughts a blur. Then she straightened up, gathering herself. Enough was enough. She would not let anyone control her any longer—not her family, not the media. She was the future Queen of Lisri. Even if she and Franco had no future, she had to protect *his* name now as much as her own family's.

CHAPTER TWENTY-FOUR

THE HAT WAS making the back of her head itch and she was hot. Far too hot. Stuffed into the royal box.

She'd left Mirabel in charge of Fiamma and the apartment and flown home just in time to ditch her bags at the house. Having changed into a dress she really didn't feel like wearing, here she was at the polo match, ten minutes before the start. Papa was playing, of course. She'd spotted him on the field already, in his hard hat, royal shirt and jodhpurs, making small talk with someone from the other team.

She raised her hand when he spotted her, and he waved dutifully as if nothing was amiss, putting on a show as usual. Ivan was on watch behind her, this time in a polo shirt. She had a sneaking suspicion that her guard was happy to be back. Things were never as crazy at the palace; no one would dare pap her with the Queen around.

She would talk to Papa later, over dinner. It was how they always did things. She was nervous about the impending conversation, but she had to stand her ground and, more importantly, she had to paint Franco in a new light. The light he deserved.

The players trotted in on their gleaming horses. The sun shone over the mountains in the distance. It should have warmed her heart like the roaring crowds—there was no place like home. But under all her fire and fresh determination the loss of him loomed heavy on her heart. He wanted nothing to do with her now—that much was clear. The photo had been the last straw… just the look on his face had said it all.

He'd loathe this royal life. There was no future for them…even if she did manage to convince her family that a few unwritten rules needed changing.

She'd tried to call him to say goodbye, and to apologise for the unwanted media attention surrounding the photo. It wasn't all bad—not like it had been after Xavier had turned her into the Ice Princess. People, it seemed, loved the hero philanthropist doctor. But that wasn't the real issue here. Franco didn't want all this—the baggage, the fuss. He'd survived a soul-crushing loss and was thriving on his own. He deserved more.

'Darling, you made it.'

Her mother swirled into the royal box in a sea-green dress, her greying hair glistening and styled. Whispers from the stands started up below, but the Queen batted her security away the second she was seated, and Adrienne couldn't help a faint smile.

'It was good of you to come, Adrienne,' her mother said, leaning in and touching her cheek to hers lightly. It was a public version of a mother-daughter kiss.

'I didn't have much of a choice,' Adrienne replied stiffly. 'But it's good to see you, Mother.'

'How are you?'

The Queen's silvery-blue eyes flashed with concern, and Adrienne struggled to hold back the tears.

She smoothed down the satin of her dress, adjusted her oversized hat. 'How do you think I am, Mother? Papa wants me to apologise...to make a statement. He wants me to pretend Franco means nothing to me so he can introduce me to...*them*.'

She gestured to the first row of seats below. A line of men in stuffy suits or too-bright shirts were toasting unknown achievements with champagne and slapping each other on the back. They'd approach her later, one by one, and probe her with questions she didn't want to answer.

'I won't do it, Mother. I won't lie.'

Her mother pursed her lips, stared at the field. The players were parading on the grass now, her father's team in the royal colours: green, orange and blue.

'You really love him, don't you? This doctor.'

Adrienne huffed a breath and leaned into her mother's soft, warm shoulder, summoning strength. 'It doesn't matter any more. He wants nothing to do with me. Can you blame him?'

Her mother stayed quiet, with her 'thinking face' on full display. They watched the match together in silence, but Adrienne barely followed the game. Papa wasn't a bad man, just overprotective, proud and stuck in his ways, and since the Xavier debacle she'd been too meek to confront him for fear of another scene that might embarrass the family.

But now the past was nipping at her heels, no matter how fast she tried to run from it. There was no choice in the matter now. No running away. Facing her family, banishing all subservient habits from her repertoire and paving a new way forward was something she had to do alone.

Franco was gone; he'd given up on her... realised he was better off without her.

Anger sizzled under her grief.

She realised now that she'd been testing Franco all this time. Every time she'd hinted at her real feelings—every time she'd let their flesh touch under a table, or met him in a kiss that spun her whole world upside down. It had all been a test to see how much fight he had. Because he'd need it if he was going to be with her.

Neither of them should have had to fight.

'Don't cry, my love,' her mother whispered.

The horses were a blur. People were looking, pointing, as they always did, and she hid her face, just as she'd done that night when Xavier had been dragged from the ballroom in front of her. Why did this feel even worse?

Xavier had fallen into her lap like a shining meteor, crashing from the sky. He taught her all about sex and red-hot sensual pleasures, showed her how to make love. Just nineteen years old when they'd met, she'd thought she'd known real love. Twelve years later it was clear she'd known nothing back then. She had never loved any man as much as she loved Franco. His happiness was everything to her. Just being in his light was the reason she threw back the covers every morning and faced each day.

Now that he didn't want her the pain was physical, gut-wrenching, as if there was a ball of steel in place of her stomach. Love was more than the act of sex. It felt as if she'd been walking through snow for years, just to reach his fire, only to have it snuffed out right in front of her.

How was she ever going to complete her oncology rotation after this, seeing him each day?

The family dinner was as she'd expected it to be. Her papa came in late, when she and her mother were already seated. Her dress felt too tight, and the cool mountain breeze gushing in through the double doors wasn't quite enough to stop the perspiration building at the back of her neck.

Ignore it. It's time.

The staff fussed around them, serving platters of food and jugs of juice, and she remained quiet at the ten-foot-long table, with her and her mother at one end, the Prince Consort at the other, and family members from the last ten centuries staring at them from the paintings on the walls.

Papa got in first—as soon as the butler was gone.

'You will give an official statement before the ball tomorrow, citing the fact that you were merely caught up in the moment...'

'I will do nothing of the sort.'

'Has our daughter not been through enough?' Her mother spoke now. She'd stood up, shoulders squared. 'We've talked about this, Alex.'

Wait. They'd talked about it already?

'Times have changed. It's a new world and Adrienne is making her place in it. We need to respect that together and honour her choices. That includes our daughter dating and even marrying any man *she* deems suitable for her hand.'

Adrienne fought the smile on her face. She hadn't been entirely sure her mother was on her side, but this was a pleasant surprise. Papa looked a little uncomfortable.

'I do not wish my girls to suffer...either of

you,' he said, clearing his throat. 'I am merely trying to help you continue the line of—'

'No, Alex,' the Queen cut in resolutely from behind his chair. 'I love you with all my heart, but…no. There is no need for announcements. We don't need to humiliate this man any more than he's already been humiliated.'

Adrienne was stunned. Her mother had taken the words right out of her mouth.

'And your daughter, Alex—you've seen what she's capable of. She and this great doctor are doing excellent work. They're role models. That is what this country needs. Let them make their own way.'

Except he doesn't want me now, she felt like saying. *The damage is done. It's too late*.

Of course she wouldn't say it.

She put her napkin down, rested her head on her hands. 'I love you, Papa, but no one should have to hide who they really are or what they really want. Not for anything. And that's the message I want to convey as Crown Princess.'

To her surprise, her father sat back in his chair and studied her quietly for a moment. Then he shook his head, hiding a smile. 'How did I know this day would come?' He paused. 'I'm proud of you, Adrienne.'

Her mother swept towards the door, beckoning Adrienne to go with her.

'Of course you're proud of her—you tell me

that all the time. It's about time you said it to her face instead. Now, come, my Princess. I'm expected in the kitchen. I've been baking the most wonderful cake for the ball tomorrow. If your Papa continues to behave, perhaps we'll save him a slice…'

CHAPTER TWENTY-FIVE

SURVIVE&THRIVE WAS THE talk of the masked ball. As the orchestra played and the guests danced and drank, everyone who came up to her had something to say about it. The app was up to over a million downloads now, and some of the patients due to take part in the trial had given more interviews—including Rosita, who was turning into somewhat of a Survive&Thrive mascot.

'What a great job.'

'You must have really impressed Dr Perretta.'

'Think about how many lives you might save!'

'What's going on with that guy, anyway?'

Of course people had been asking her about him, too. Every time someone said his name her heart sank.

Adrienne fixed her hair around her mask in the lavish bathroom, resting her hands for a moment on the cool tiles, wishing she could escape this silly thing. Then again, flying back to Naples, to Franco's inevitable disdain, was not a comforting prospect either. She still hadn't heard from him. She'd tried to call, but his phone had either rung out or he'd denied her calls. Frustration ate at her insides. And she hadn't slept properly since she'd left Naples.

At least Papa seemed amicable, she thought, once she was back in the opulent ballroom, with its candles flickering from every wall. Ten-foot-high paintings of royal ancestors peered over the evening's entertainment, and all the Dukes and Barons and Lords she was trying to avoid. She knew they'd try it on even without being encouraged by her father.

Not that she could tell who anyone was behind their masks. There were so many people here, their faces all obscured or partly hidden.

'Excuse me, Adrienne? Might I have a word?'

'So sorry—have to go.'

She gathered her floor-length gown and turned away from the oncoming Count, watching Papa work the room with his crowd of aristocratic cronies on the side-lines.

He'd conceded last night—in the kitchen, no less—that perhaps he'd pushed her a little too far. He'd even apologised for what had happened with Xavier all those years ago and promised to support her going forward. She'd resisted the urge to say *Too little, too late*—something about the look her mother had given her had stopped her in her tracks.

Whatever the Queen wanted was his wish too, he'd said. He'd also agreed that her mother's cake was the best he'd tasted in a long time.

'Princess Adrienne?'

The male voice behind her caused a lurch of nausea. When would they all just *stop*? The music was loud now, and she could barely hear what the man was saying. He was standing some three feet away, a picture of masculine elegance in the spotlights. His mask was all black feathers, with a crow's beak protruding in her direction, and it concealed his entire face. His suit looked like the stuff of a talented royal tailor. She had to admit he looked damn fine in it. He was looking her up and down in silent appreciation, and whereas usually she'd turn the other way something drew her closer.

'I have to warn you, if you're about to ask me to dance, or if you're about to try and woo me, it won't work. My heart is taken,' she heard herself say.

Better to warn him straight away—so he knew. It was going to take her a long time to get over Franco, even if they'd never even really got started.

Over his shoulder, she caught her mother watching with interest.

The crow stepped even closer. 'Who stole your heart?' he asked.

She realised the crowd around her had gone quiet. People were whispering, watching her, and the spotlights felt hot on the satin fabric of her dress. She held her head high, knowing Papa was probably watching too. And all the other men who wanted a piece of her.

'If you must know, his name is Franco Perretta,' she said, directly to the crow in front of her. 'You might have seen a photo of us, which was taken without our permission? He saved a girl's life that day.'

The crow cocked his head. All eyes were on them both now. She might as well keep going.

'He's a leader,' she proclaimed, squaring her shoulders. 'He's funny, and kind, and he always speaks the truth—right from here.'

She clamped a fist to her heart, and the crow's eyes narrowed inside the slits of the mask.

Sucking in a breath, she prayed for her voice not to tremble. 'He tells a story like no one else I know, and if he loves you, he loves you *fiercely*, with *everything* he has. He's the greatest doctor I know. The most passionate, inspiring human I know. Any woman would be lucky to have him. And we're going to save a lot more lives together…just as soon as I can get out of here.'

The crow was silent for a long time, watching her as her heart pounded in a galloping beat. The music played on softly, but no one was speaking.

Maybe she'd said too much?

Swallowing her nerves, Adrienne almost turned to hurry from the room.

But the crow's hand caught her bare arm, just

below the sleeve of her gown. The touch made her reel in swift recognition.

Gasping, she reached for his mask. 'Franco!' she cried as it dropped to the floor and feathers scattered across the tiles.

Her hands flew to her mouth. She blinked, not sure whether to laugh, cry or be furious.

'Franco,' she said again on an exhalation. It came out as more of a sob this time.

He pulled her in close, firm against his chest, cradling the back of her head and shielding her from the onlookers. Her hands found the lapels of his jacket, and her nostrils sucked in his familiar scent as if it was a life force.

'That was quite a speech,' he whispered in her ear, tangling one hand in her hair.

How was this real? Her legs felt as if they might fail beneath her.

'What are you doing here?'

'Your mother invited me.'

What?

He took her shoulders and she watched his green eyes dart around the room as people lifted their masks to get a better look at him—at *them*. Someone started clapping. Then someone else— the Count—followed suit.

'I couldn't refuse the Queen, could I?'

To Adrienne's utter shock, her mother raised her hand at Franco in greeting, and then the entire room erupted in an enormous cheer. He turned back to her, grazing her lips with his sea-green eyes. Then he swept her face to his in with one gentle, insistent palm and kissed her.

The room disappeared. The music grew louder, but Adrienne felt as if she was dreaming. She let him lead her towards her mother...watched him bow to her and smile, and laugh about something. Then, to her utter shock, she watched Papa give him the kind of handshake he usually reserved for royalty.

Surreal. She couldn't imagine what it must be like for Franco.

Later, out in the rose garden, he explained how her mother had summoned him, told him he was free to date Adrienne if he felt the same way *she* felt. She'd said she would come down hard on any publication that dared to pester them too much or darken either of their names.

'And the Baron...?'

'I wasn't ever concerned that you had feelings for him,' he said, cupping her face.

The Lisri moonlight accentuated every line and angle of his handsome face as he caressed her cheek, and she couldn't wait to get him alone, away from all these people, behind closed doors. Could she even dare to hope for a future for them now? So many questions were hanging on her lips, but he seemed to have all the answers.

'I was angry at myself more than you, for

thinking that my privacy and the chip on my shoulder about my lack of blue blood were more important than the work we have to do together... the future we might build. You're my inspiration. You're standing up for the life you really want, and changing so many other people's lives while you're at it.'

'I don't care about your lineage, but I know your privacy is important to you, Franco. You hate the spotlight. And being with me...that's a lot to take on. Even if I don't take the crown for another thirty or forty years!'

'Well, I guess that will give me plenty of time to get used to it,' he said, making her heart hammer under her dress. He was serious.

A lazy smile stretched his face. His kiss was all the answer she needed. He lingered, tilting her chin towards the moonlight, touching his lips to hers as if savouring the moment.

'I've had some pretty efficient defences up for a very long time,' he said. 'I didn't expect a royal superstar to blaze in and turn my life upside down.'

She smiled in his arms. 'I do apologise.'

'I forgive you,' he said as a firework lit up the sky from the palace rooftop. 'And I love you so much. I know it won't all be smooth sailing—far from it. Even if your mother does come down hard on the media in our defence.'

'Not as hard as I will if anyone dares attack my future Prince,' she told him, eyes narrowed.

She knew without a doubt that she'd have no problem speaking her mind about anything from now on. The press would always find something to talk about. The Ice Princess had melted, after all. They just had to ensure they were talking about the right things. Their work. Their values. Their goals.

Franco trailed a finger up her arm, along the seam of her dress to the flesh of her cleavage, then to her lips. 'I kind of like the sound of being your Prince,' he said, and breathlessly she sank into his kiss, letting herself fall a little further.

Whatever happened now, with Franco at her side, and her country cheering her on, she would be ready.

CHAPTER TWENTY-SIX

Six months later

'FRANCO! FRANCO, HOW do I look?'

Rosita hurried over to him in the garden, with Adrienne's cat, Fiamma, under one arm. Her loose, silky black hair swung around her shoulders, and she looked a picture of health in her rose-coloured satin dress.

'Do I look OK for the rehearsal photos?'

Franco stopped in his tracks with Benni, admiring his radiant Survive&Thrive ambassador and patient as she stood in the light of the flaming torches circling the icy lake. She'd become quite close to Adrienne, and she was gaining a following of her own.

'You and Alina are the most beautiful bridesmaids a man and a crown princess could wish for,' he said. 'What are you worried about?'

Rosita beamed at him and snuggled her face into the cat's fur. She'd taken full ownership of him lately, since Adrienne had been so busy, and he had an inkling the responsibility had given her a reason to get up each morning. She had a thousand reasons now.

He watched her take his niece's hand. Alina had been so excited ever since his brother and his family had flown in on the royal jet. Meeting the Queen and his bride-to-be the Crown Princess all in one day, then touring the royal palace with the Prince Consort was a story she'd be telling for months.

'I think Rosita's worried about her hair,' Benni said to him as they watched the girls hurry towards the others, past the twinkling fairy lights that had made a dream world of the royal palace's garden.

'But it's grown back beautifully,' Franco told him. 'And she didn't lose half the hair she might have done if we hadn't got her on that trial.'

They'd all been flown here to Lisri for the wedding—every one of them at Adrienne's insistence. Mr Geordano was here, Diodoro and his partner, and Candice. And the housekeeper Mirabel, who flushed every time she saw him, as if she was still embarrassed over asking him if he had an appointment that time after Adrienne's motorcycle accident.

It seemed everyone was thriving since the Crown Princess had arrived at the Institute. Even little Emma, the girl they'd rescued on the beach that day, was here with her mother. Adrienne had invited everyone who'd made an impression on her since she'd met him, which was so typically *her*.

It was going to be the royal wedding of the century. This was only the rehearsal, so tomorrow he'd probably be sick with nerves. But of course there was no way he'd show it. He'd been more nervous pulling the ring out when he'd proposed, in case she said no.

He'd taken her out on the yacht, just the two of them, two months ago. Someone had told him the dolphins had come back, and she'd cried when she saw them. She'd cried even more when he'd dropped to one knee and the whole pod had leapt from the water in their wake, as if they knew they had to impress her, too.

'Franco!'

Adrienne was sweeping down the steps now, with a backdrop of dramatic stormy clouds behind her, the Queen and Prince Consort Alex either side of her. 'Franco, we need a photo,' she said.

He was struck by her beauty all over again. The huge diamond on her finger looked as if it was on fire, reflecting the torches all around them.

Benni nudged him, bringing him back to earth.

'You got the girl of your dreams,' he reminded him, and it crossed Franco's mind, for just the fastest flicker of a second, that his brother had never said that about Luci.

But maybe he'd just been too young when he'd proposed to her. Too young to think too much about the future and what he really wanted from life. He knew now. He'd never thought about anything as hard as he'd had to think about becoming half of Lisri's new power couple. He'd thought about Luci the night before he'd proposed to Adrienne. In a way, his love for her had brought him here. He hoped somewhere, somehow, she was at peace with his decision.

Now, in her ankle length silver-grey dress, with a wreath of roses and a snug faux-fur-lined shawl, Adrienne looked every inch the Crown Princess. An outdoor winter wedding was something different, but it wasn't as if she'd ever have settled for something so pedestrian as Lisri's cathedral.

Something in her eyes made her look panicked for a second as she took his hands. Her father flashed his gaze towards him, then to the Queen, then cleared his throat.

'How about a photograph of Franco and the Queen and I first?' he asked. 'Benni, Aimee and Marco, too,' he added, beckoning them over. 'We all know you're like royalty in Naples.'

Prince Alex winked, to his surprise. He'd never seen Adrienne's father wink at anyone before. It was nice to see how much he'd lightened up lately. Maybe he was happy to be unburdened of the weight of his own redundant rules, now they were being broken on a daily basis.

Adrienne dropped a kiss to her father's cheek. 'That's a great idea,' she said. Then she whispered, 'Thank you, Papa.'

Adrienne beamed and Franco smoothed his tailored jacket for the photo. It was emblazoned with the royal crest on the pocket. He was still getting used to how things were around the royal family of Lisri. It was a life he never could have imagined, even though they'd been living in Naples, continuing much as normal, albeit with a few obligations on certain weekends back here.

Further down the line, when Adrienne became Queen, they'd move here to the palace, to a home on the grounds they were designing together. He would be ready for it. Ready for the life they were already building.

'Our suite is all ready for tomorrow. I saw the chambermaids going in with champagne and candles,' she whispered once their photos were done, sweeping him to one side while the photographers fussed and snapped more photos of the guests behind them.

He drew her in, pressed a kiss to her forehead, and she shuddered in his arms suddenly. 'I am nervous,' she said. 'More nervous about that than everyone watching us walk down the aisle, when we'll be televised around the world.'

'Why?' He almost laughed as he touched a hand to her flushed cheek, letting the faux fur shawl tickle his fingers. 'There won't be any cameras on our wedding night.' He smiled, leaning in. 'How will I survive tonight in our separate rooms?'

People were watching, but he was used to that now. She bit her lip, adjusting his tie, her mouth an inch from his. 'You'll just have to try. And tomorrow I will worship every part of you, for as long as I deem fit, as your wife,' she said, touching her lips to his in a way that made him want to pull her in by her hips in front of everyone. 'Over and over and over and—'

'Adrienne? We need you and the Survive&Thrive guests next. One for the website. Are you ready?'

Adrienne gave him a look that only he could see—one that spoke volumes about the lack of sleep they would both be experiencing on their wedding night. He rooted his feet to the floor as she floated back towards her guests, and he caught Rosita grinning at him knowingly.

Damn, he would have to get better at withholding the PDAs—but at least the press were only writing positive things about them now, portraying them as role models in love, career aspirations and everything else.

He made his way back to Benni, Aimee and his father. Benni slapped him on the back. 'Hey, Franco, we were just talking about the royal wedding dolls they've made of you both. Did you know Dad's ordered a hundred already, to give as gifts to the kids at the institute?'

Franco rolled his eyes. OK, so some things would take more getting used to than others, going forward. But they had support and allies all around them now. For ever with the Crown Princess of Lisri was going to be one hell of a ride…but he couldn't wait to get started.

*****

If you enjoyed this story, check out these other great reads from Becky Wicks

White Christmas with Her Millionaire Doc
Fling with the Children's Heart Doctor
Falling Again for the Animal Whisperer
Enticed by Her Island Billionaire

All available now!